D0278810

"I wish all Holmesian pastiche could be as honest, as knowledgeable, as enthusiastic and as well written – in short, as good – as these children's books."

THE SHERLOCK HOLMES SOCIETY OF LONDON

Other Baker Street Boys adventures:

THE CASE OF THE DISAPPEARING DETECTIVE

ANTHONY READ

illustrated by

DAVID FRANKLAND

WALKER
BOOKS

For Elliot, Jack, Miranda and Oliver

This is a work of fiction. Names, characters, places and incidents
are either the product of the author's imagination or, if real, used
fictitiously. All statements, activities, stunts, descriptions, information
and material of any other kind contained herein are included for
entertainment purposes only and should not be relied on for
accuracy or replicated as they may result in injury.

First published 2005 by Walker Books Ltd
87 Vauxhall Walk, London SE11 5HJ

This edition published 2012.

2 4 6 8 10 9 7 5 3 1

Text © 2005 Anthony Read
Illustrations © 2005 David Frankland

The right of Anthony Read and David Frankland to be identified as author
and illustrator respectively of this work has been asserted by them in
accordance with the Copyright, Designs and Patents Act 1988

This book has been typeset in ITC Garamond

Printed and bound in Italy by Grafica Veneta S.p.A.

All rights reserved. No part of this book may be reproduced, transmitted or
stored in an information retrieval system in any form or by any means,
graphic, electronic or mechanical, including photocopying, taping and
recording, without prior written permission from the publisher.

British Library Cataloguing in Publication Data:
a catalogue record for this book
is available from the British Library

ISBN 978-1-4063-3634-4

www.walker.co.uk

CONTENTS

THE IRREGULARS ON THE TRAIL

The fog wrapped itself round Wiggins like a dirty, yellow fleece. It was what Victorian Londoners called "a real pea-souper", fed by the smoke of a million coal fires pouring out of a million chimneypots. It may have been the same colour as pea soup, but it had a very different flavour. The taste in Wiggins's mouth was sooty and sharp. He had covered his mouth and nose with his scarf, and there was a dark circle where he had been breathing through it. His throat was sore and his eyes smarted. He shivered with the damp cold, and wished he did not have to be out on a day like this.

Although it was only early afternoon, the fog was so thick that he could not see halfway across the street. People passing by him on the pavement materialized like ghosts and then were swallowed up again in the gloom. The sounds of the traffic were muffled: the clinking of harness, the clopping of horses' hooves and the clatter of iron-rimmed carriage wheels echoed dully from the cobblestones. The jangle of music from a barrel organ and the cries of the hot-chestnut seller on the next corner seemed to come from nowhere. Wiggins could not see the man or his barrow, but the whiff of the chestnuts roasting on a coke brazier wafted past his nostrils. It was a delicious smell. Wiggins's empty stomach rumbled. A bag of hot, sweet chestnuts would ease his hunger, and warm his hands at the same time.

It was very tempting, but he could not leave his post. Mr Holmes had told him to watch a certain house and look out for the man who was staying there.

"It is a matter of great importance," the famous detective had told him that morning, looking very serious. "Of national importance. Keep your eyes on that house at all times. Take note of anyone coming or going. If our man leaves,

I want to know exactly where he goes, and who he meets."

"Yes, sir, Mr Holmes," Wiggins replied, touching his black billycock hat in a salute. "You can rely on me."

"I know I can, Wiggins. That's why I'm entrusting you with this mission."

"And the other Boys," Wiggins continued. "We're all at your command."

"Excellent. But take no chances. This man may be dangerous."

"We'll be careful, sir."

"Good. He must not know he is being watched."

"No, sir."

Mr Holmes produced a shiny silver shilling, and handed it over with a nod. Wiggins thanked him, and slipped it into his pocket.

"You will be in charge, as usual," Mr Holmes concluded. "I leave it to you to organize the rest of my Irregulars."

Wiggins grinned. Sherlock Holmes liked to call his band of urchins "The Baker Street Irregulars". He said they were "the unofficial

Baker Street division of the detective police force". When they were working on a case, they sometimes used that name. But generally they called themselves "The Baker Street Boys". In fact, three of the seven "Boys" were girls, but none of them seemed to mind being called "Boys". There had only been boys in the gang when they started out, and they had chosen to keep the name when the girls joined them, one by one.

Wiggins was the eldest – he thought he was about fourteen, but he wasn't sure. He had been living on the streets for as long as he could remember, ever since his home had burnt to the ground in a fire. The rest of his family – his mother, father, sisters and brothers – had all died in the flames. Even now, years later, he still had dreams about that dreadful night. Generally, though, he was a bright and cheerful lad, with a ready grin and sharp eyes under his tangle of dark hair. He had learned to take care of himself, and of his friends. The other Boys all looked up to him and accepted him as their captain, although that was not to say they always obeyed him without arguing.

Fighting off the pangs of hunger, Wiggins turned up the collar of his threadbare old coat and huddled into the shelter of the doorway that was his observation post. He pulled a battered old watch from his inside pocket and checked it for the umpteenth time, scarcely able to believe it was still only three o'clock. He was growing bored and weary, and his eyelids were just beginning to droop when he heard the noise of bolts being drawn back. At once he was wide awake again.

A pale shaft of light spilled on to the pavement as the door he was watching opened, then a man's shadow fell across it. The man was big, and seemed even bigger because of the heavy greatcoat he was wearing, with its thick collar of black, curly fur, and a black, broad-brimmed hat pulled low over his eyes. He was carrying a stout walking stick with a large silver knob at the top, holding it like a club.

Wiggins shrank back out of sight.

I wouldn't like to cross *him*, he thought. I bet he'd smash you with that stick if you just looked at him wrong.

The man peered carefully to the left and right. He hardly noticed Wiggins, lounging in the shadows. Or the other Boys, hanging about in different places on the street. They were just scruffy children in ragged clothes, as much a part of the street scene as lampposts and red pillar boxes.

The door closed behind the man. As the bolts were drawn again from the inside, he strode away, passing so close to Wiggins that the young detective could have reached out and touched him. If he had wanted to – which he didn't. But Wiggins did get a close look at the man's face: the skin was coarse and ruddy, the nose had been broken and there was a white scar running down one cheek. His mouth was partly hidden by a heavy black moustache that turned up at the ends, but in the half-light it looked cruel. His eyes, shaded by his hat, seemed narrow and mean.

Wiggins shivered again, and this time it was not from the cold. He slipped out of his doorway and followed the man, walking a few paces behind. He did not dare get too close, but he had to take care not to lose him in the fog. As he passed the entrance porch of a darkened house, he nodded to another Boy, Beaver, who was lurking there. Beaver emerged and followed a little behind him, as backup in case anything went wrong.

As Wiggins's deputy, Beaver always seemed to be following him. If Wiggins was a born leader, Beaver was a born follower. He was about one year younger than Wiggins, but nearly as big, and much stronger – he was easily the strongest of the Boys and could lift surprisingly heavy weights, which was sometimes very useful. He got his name from the hat he always wore – an old-fashioned sort of top hat, known as a "beaver" because it was made from beaver fur. He had discovered it in someone's rubbish and taken an instant fancy to it. (Most of the Boys wore clothes they had found among people's cast-offs.) The name suited him, anyway. He looked a bit like a beaver, and he was just as hard-working and amiable as that furry creature.

Beaver's father was a seaman, who had sailed away to the East and never come back. His mother had deserted him soon afterwards. Beaver still dreamed that his father would turn up again one day, laden with gifts from his travels, but even he knew that it was a vain hope. He had been adopted by a shopkeeper, who fed him on scraps and made him slave from early morning till late at night and sleep on a pile of sacks under the counter. One day, Beaver had gone out on an errand and never found his way back. He had not deliberately run away – it had just sort of happened. Beaver was that kind of chap. Wiggins had found him and taken him under his wing. Together they had become the first of the Baker Street Boys.

The little procession – the big man, Wiggins and Beaver – made its way along the street. After a few yards, they passed a girl standing on the edge of the kerb, selling small bunches of flowers from a tray hung around her neck.

Rosie was another of the Boys – a pretty girl aged about twelve, but who looked much younger. Wiggins signalled with his hand that she was to stay there and not follow. Two Boys could pass unnoticed, but any more might not. Rosie tossed her head in disappointment, making her fair curls fall across her delicate face. But she brightened up when an old gentleman approached her, smiling kindly, and handed over two pennies for a nosegay.

As Wiggins reached the hot-chestnut seller's barrow on the street corner, the temptation became too much. He could not resist stretching out his hand and helping himself to a chestnut. It was so hot he had to toss it from hand to hand to stop it burning his fingers. The hot-chestnut seller was busy serving a customer, and didn't see him. But when Beaver helped himself too, he was caught in the act.

"Oi!" the hot-chestnut seller bellowed. "You! Come back 'ere, you rascal!"

Hearing the shout, the man they were tailing half turned and looked back – straight at the two Boys. Wiggins thought fast. If the hot-chestnut seller grabbed them and handed them over, they wouldn't be able to follow him. There was only one thing to do.

"Run for it!" he cried to Beaver. "This way!"

And they raced off, passing one on either side of the big man.

A few yards further on, they took cover behind a stack of boxes outside a greengrocer's shop.

"Oh, lor!" Wiggins panted. "I hope we ain't lost him."

"Sorry, Wiggins," Beaver replied. He looked down at the chestnut he was still holding, then shrugged, pulled off the shell and took a bite. As he nibbled at it with his two big front teeth, he looked more like a beaver than ever. "Mmmm … that's good…"

Wiggins paused for a moment, then peeled his own chestnut and stuffed it into his mouth. "Yeah," he agreed. "Very nice."

Beaver thought as he chewed. His face cleared. "It'll be all right," he said. "He's gotta come past here."

"Unless he crosses the road or takes a cab."

Beaver's face fell again. "Oh. Yeah… Hadn't thought of that. Oh dear."

"Hang on. Here he comes."

They heard the sound of the metal tip of the big man's stick clacking on the pavement, then the man himself appeared. To the Boys' horror, he stopped in front of the shop, barely a yard from their hiding place. Wiggins put his finger to his lips, and clutched Beaver's sleeve in case he decided to run. But the man had not seen them. Tossing a penny to the greengrocer, he picked up an apple from the neat display outside the shop, rubbed it on his sleeve to polish it and took a bite. Then he set off again at a brisk pace. Wiggins and Beaver followed at a safe distance.

For a couple of minutes, they stayed on the man's tail. Sometimes they lost sight of him for a moment, as swirls of fog came between them, but they could hear the sound of his stick, so they knew he was still there. Then, suddenly, the clacking of the stick stopped. They looked at each other, then cautiously edged forward. A slight breeze lifted the fog a little, so they could see the pavement ahead of them. There was no sign of their man.

"Oh, no," Beaver groaned. "Where's he gone?"

"I dunno," Wiggins replied. "Unless... Look – see that little alleyway." He pointed to a gap between two buildings, so narrow that if he were to stretch his arms out he could have touched both walls at once.

"You reckon?" Beaver asked.

"Gotta be. Ain't nowhere else he could have gone. Careful, now. If he sees us following..."

They crept into the alleyway. It had plain brick walls on either side, with no openings of any sort. After a few feet, it turned to the right. Wiggins tiptoed to the corner and peeped cautiously round. There was no one there. And no way out, except for an iron door set into the end wall.

"He must have gone through there," Beaver whispered.

"He can't have. It's barred and bolted from this side."

And indeed it was. Two heavy bolts at the top and bottom were secured with padlocks. Across the middle of the door was a thick iron bar, fastened with an even bigger padlock.

"We was wrong," Beaver said. "He couldn't have come down here after all." He reached out and tested the door. It was solid. So were the padlocks.

Wiggins looked around, examining the rest of the alleyway for any sign of a secret entrance or trapdoor. There was none. Then he spotted something on the ground. "He *was* here!" he exclaimed. "Look."

He held up what he had found. It was an apple core.

Beaver looked puzzled. "What does that prove?" he asked.

"It's fresh," Wiggins told him. "It ain't even started to turn brown. It's the apple what our man was eating."

THE SECRET CELLAR

"What's that s'posed to be?" Queenie asked scornfully.

"It's a apple core, stupid," Shiner told her, equally scornful.

Shiner was Queenie's younger brother, which gave him the right to be cheeky to her – or so he thought. Queenie, of course, thought differently.

"Stupid yourself," she retorted. "Any more of your lip and you'll get a thick ear."

Shiner pulled a face and stuck his tongue out at her.

"Or bed with no supper," she went on – a threat that could usually be relied on to shut Shiner up.

He scowled and went into a sulk.

"Now then, now then!" Wiggins intervened.

He pointed to the apple core, sitting on a grubby handkerchief on the table. The rest of the Boys were gathered around it. "That," he announced solemnly, "ain't just an apple core. That is *evidence*. Mr Holmes his self says so."

"Cor!" said Rosie, the little flower girl, gazing in awe at the withered, brown object.

"No, not a core – evidence!" chortled Sparrow, the youngest and smallest of the Boys, pleased with his own joke.

Sparrow's ambition for when he grew up was to be a comedian at the music hall where he sometimes worked as a call boy, telling the performers when they were due on stage and generally helping out. For practice, he was always making jokes. Occasionally they were funny; sometimes they were so awful that the other Boys threw things at him. This time they just groaned.

The Boys were all gathered in their secret headquarters, which they called HQ for short. This was a cellar, beneath a derelict and decaying old building, reached through a narrow passage off a side street near Baker Street itself. Its entrance was so well hidden that no one would guess it was there. This was where they lived together, free from adult interference, looking after themselves with occasional help from understanding friends, like Dr Watson, Sherlock Holmes's companion.

They had furnished their HQ with all sorts of bits and pieces they had found on streets and dumps – stuff that people had thrown out. An old kitchen table stood in the middle of the room. It had lost a leg, but they had propped up that corner with a thick piece of timber, so the top was nearly level. Some things they had made, out of pieces of wood and old fruit boxes. The best piece of furniture was a wonderful arm-chair, which Wiggins had made for himself out of parts of other chairs, old cushions and pieces of wood and string. No one else was allowed to use it. When he had a particularly knotty prob-lem to solve, Wiggins would sit in it and think, just like his hero, Sherlock Holmes. And, like Sherlock Holmes, he would suck on a big, curly pipe to help him think – though of course he never put any tobacco in it. He had tried once, but it had made him cough so much when he lit it that he had thought his lungs would burst, and the others had said his face had turned a very interesting shade of green.

On the wall above the chair hung a picture of Mr Holmes, which Queenie had found in a magazine. She had carefully cut it out and put it in an old frame, as a present to Wiggins. For herself she had framed a picture of Queen Victoria, looking very regal, with a small crown on her head. The Queen was celebrating her Diamond Jubilee that year, marking sixty years on the throne, and there were pictures of her everywhere in London. Queenie could hardly imagine what it would be like to even *live* for sixty years, but she knew it was a very, very long time. Like almost everyone in the country, she was pleased and proud that their Queen was still reigning over them.

Queenie was the leading girl among the Boys. She was nearly as old as Wiggins, and could be just as bossy. The younger ones looked on her like a mother, which sometimes annoyed her. She would have liked to go out with Wiggins and

Beaver, doing jobs for Mr Holmes and having adventures, but the others needed her to look after them.

It was Queenie who cooked the Boys' food on the old, black stove that had been in the cellar when they first moved in. None of the others could cook like Queenie, though sometimes they tried. Beaver had once managed to burn the bottom right out of her best pan, and Wiggins's attempt at scrambled eggs had been so rubbery that not even Shiner had been able to eat it. Queenie suspected that Wiggins had done it on purpose – she said she couldn't see how *anybody* could make eggs tough. Queenie was an excellent cook. She could turn a few scrag-ends of meat and a bag of old vegetables – begged from a friendly butcher and greengrocer at the end of the day – into a delicious stew.

Queenie's mother had taught her how to cook when Queenie was quite small, and when her mother had become ill, Queenie had taken over the cooking for the family. That was when she had started looking after other people, and it had become a habit. Her mother, who had been very fond of books, had also taught her to read. When her mother was very ill, Queenie would read to her as she lay in her bed. Queenie still loved reading, and did her best to teach the other Boys. None of them, not even Wiggins, were as good as she was, and some of them found it hard, but Queenie persevered with the lessons, telling them that being able to read would always prove useful.

After Queenie's mother died, her father had started drinking heavily, and beating her. When he started beating her little brother, Albert, too, they had run away, though they had nowhere to go. Beaver had found them sheltering in a door-way, afraid to look for help in case they were separated, or sent back to their drunken father. They had been relieved and delighted to find a new home with the Baker Street Boys. Soon after, Albert had found a job – as a shoeshine boy at Paddington railway station – and with it a new name, "Shiner", which suited him much better than "Albert".

Shiner was now about eleven or twelve years old, a born rebel with a temper that often got him – and sometimes the other Boys – into trouble. He could be stubborn and selfish, but he had his good side, too: he was brave in the face of danger, and he could always be relied on to see any job through, no matter how hard it was.

Shiner was a quick lad with sharp ears, good at listening to his customers as he polished their boots and shoes, and picking up useful gossip. He had once overheard a respectable-looking business-man (who, incidentally, had been wearing an expensive pair of elastic-sided brown boots) telling another man about hiding stolen jewels in the station's left-luggage office. Shiner had reported this to Wiggins. Wiggins had reported it to Mr Holmes. And Mr Holmes had been able to catch the thief, recover the jewels and hand both over to Inspector Lestrade of Scotland Yard.

Shiner had basked in everyone's praise at this triumph. But he had spoiled things by not wanting to share the reward with the other Boys. Queenie, however, had soon put a stop to that, and they had all enjoyed a blow-out feast that left them feeling full for days.

* * *

Now, Wiggins was explaining about finding the apple core, and how the big man had vanished without trace. "Like a puff of smoke," he said.

"I seen that done at the theatre," chipped in Sparrow. "They has this powder in a little tray, and when you put a spark to it, it goes up in a big flash."

"What's that got to do with it?" Rosie asked.

"It makes a lot of smoke as well. And while the audience is still half blinded by the flash, the lady what's got to disappear nips out and nobody sees her go 'cos of the smoke."

"There weren't no flash," said Beaver solemnly. "We'd have seen it. Right, Wiggins?"

"What you on about?" Wiggins sounded exasperated. "Course there weren't no flash. Nor no smoke, neither."

"There was the fog…"

"Beaver!"

"Sorry."

"This weren't no conjuring trick. Mr Holmes said it was very interesting."

"Was he cross with you for losing the man?" Rosie asked.

"No," Wiggins replied. "I thought he would be, but when I told him what happened, and showed him that –" he pointed to the apple core "– he just said it was very interesting and that we done really well."

"I can't see how," said Queenie. "What's he want us to do now?"

"He says we're to keep up the good work, and he gave me another bob. Look." He held up another shiny shilling, then dropped it into the cracked china toby jug on a shelf near the stove, where they kept their meagre savings. The jug was shaped like the head of a man wearing a three-cornered hat and a black mask across his eyes. Wiggins said it was Dick Turpin, the famous highwayman. Queenie thought it was funny to have a robber looking after their money, but Wiggins always laughed and said there was nobody better.

"Well, we must be doin' somethin' right," said Shiner, cheering up at the chink of the money in the jug and the thought of the food it might buy.

"We've gotta keep looking out for that man,

and anybody else what goes in and out of that house," Wiggins told them.

A sudden shout from the doorway made them all turn round.

"I seen him! I seen him, just now!"

Gertie, the last of the Baker Street Boys, had just pushed her way in through the sacking sheet that hung over the cellar entrance. Her green eyes were sparkling with excitement.

"Where? Where d'you see him?" Wiggins demanded.

"Out there, in the street. I was holdin' this horse's head—"

"You can't hold horses' heads!" Shiner interrupted. "That's a lad's job."

"I 'spect they thought she *was* a lad," said Rosie.

And indeed Gertie did look like a boy, with her ginger hair cropped short and ragged trousers reaching just below her knees, and she was well able to hold horses' heads to stop them straying while their carriages were parked at the kerbside. She grinned, pleased by what Rosie had said, and continued. "I was holdin' this horse's head – a grey, it was, with a lovely long mane – when our man comes along and stands on the kerb right by me."

The others gasped.

"Right by me," Gertie repeated dramatically. "Then he hails a cab."

"Where to? Did you hear where he was going?" asked Wiggins.

"Clear as a bell. 'Driver,' says he, 'take me to Paddington railroad station, quick as you can!'"

"Paddington!" exclaimed Shiner.

"Railroad?" Beaver puzzled. "Why'd he say that?"

"Why were you talkin' in that funny voice?" asked Queenie.

"'Cos that's how he talked. You know what I reckon?" Gertie cried triumphantly. "I reckon he's a Yankee!"

"An American, you say?" Sherlock Holmes nodded his head thoughtfully.

"That's what Gertie thinks," Wiggins replied. He was standing before the great detective in his rooms at 221b Baker Street, twisting his hat nervously in his hands.

Dr Watson sat near by, an encouraging smile on his friendly face, stroking his full moustache as he listened to what Wiggins had to say.

"And has Gertie ever heard an American speak before?" Mr Holmes asked.

"I dunno."

"Could he, perhaps, have been an Irishman?"

"Oh no, sir," Wiggins replied confidently. "She knows what an Irishman sounds like. There's lots of Irishmen in London. 'Sides, her dad was an Irishman."

"And there is the matter of terminology," Dr Watson added.

"Eh? I beg pardon, sir?"

"Names," Mr Holmes said. "The use of 'railroad' instead of 'railway'."

"Precisely," said Dr Watson. "'Railroad' is an American term."

"Thank you, Watson," Mr Holmes replied sarcastically. "We are aware of that."

"Yes, of course. Just trying to help, old chap."

Mr Holmes snorted impatiently. "This requires a great deal of thought," he said. Striding across the room, he picked up his violin from a shelf and plucked its strings to check that it was in tune.

Dr Watson got hurriedly to his feet and made for the door.

"I … er … I have to visit a patient," he stammered. "Come along, Wiggins. We'll leave Mr Holmes to his deliberations."

As they descended the stairs on their way out they heard the screech of the violin's first notes.

Dr Watson looked at Wiggins with a pained expression on his face. "I always enjoy a good tune," he said. "But this modern music…"

Wiggins nodded sympathetically. "Still," he said, "if it helps him think…"

"Oh, it does that, all right. Can't for the life of me see how, but it seems to work for him. Sometimes he'll play for hours. In a world of his own. Then he'll suddenly lay down the violin, smile, and say 'I have it, Watson!'"

"Brilliant!"

"Yes. He has a remarkable brain. Quite remarkable."

Dr Watson closed the shiny, black front door behind them, settled his top hat firmly on his head and bade Wiggins goodbye.

"Should I come back tomorrow for more orders?" Wiggins asked.

"Yes," the Doctor replied. "Yes, why don't you come back in the morning." And he marched away down the street.

Wiggins stood for a moment, listening to the sound of the violin coming from inside the house. The fog had thinned slightly, and when he looked up at Mr Holmes's window he could see his shadow on the blind, playing his unearthly music. As Wiggins turned away, however, he realized that he was not the only one watching that window. There was a closed carriage standing at the kerbside, with a small but distinct letter "M" painted on the door. Inside it, he could just make out the gaunt figure of a middle-aged man with a large, dome-like, bald head, his sunken eyes fixed intently on the silhouette of the detective. There was something evil about the man, and Wiggins felt a chill as he looked at him. For a moment, a cold smile flickered across the man's cadaverous features, then he rapped with his cane on the roof of the carriage, and it pulled away into the gloom.

THE MOST DANGEROUS MAN
IN LONDON

The fog had lifted a little next morning, but the light was still gloomy as Wiggins made his way back to 221b Baker Street.

He had already posted the Boys on look-out duty around the streets, but there was no sign of movement from the big man's house. He had sent Shiner to his work at Paddington Station with strict instructions to watch out for the man there.

"He won't be hard to spot," Wiggins had told him. "He's so big, you'd see his head well above the crowd."

"Don't worry," Shiner had answered keenly. "I don't miss much on that station. If he's there, I'll see him."

"Good lad. Off you go, then."

Shiner had saluted and hotfooted it to Paddington. Wiggins had checked over his troops and then headed for Baker Street. On the way, he had passed Rosie, just returning from the market at Covent Garden with a full tray of fresh little flowers to sell. He had asked her to patrol the street near the alley with the iron door, to watch for any comings or goings there.

Confident that he had everything covered, he arrived on Mr Holmes's doorstep. But before he tugged the shiny brass bell pull, he took a careful look around, to make sure the sinister "M" was not watching. Only when he was certain that he wasn't did he ring. The door was opened, even before the bell had stopped tinkling, by a boy who was about the same age and height as Wiggins but very different in appearance.

Billy was the pageboy employed by Mrs Hudson, the landlady, to answer the door, show visitors in and run errands and take messages for her and the people who, like Sherlock Holmes, rented sets of rooms in the house. He was dressed in a typical pageboy's uniform: trousers with a broad, red stripe down the side and a tight jacket, with two rows of brass buttons running up the front, fastened right to the neck. When he went out on an errand, he wore a little pillbox hat at a jaunty angle, held on by a piece of elastic under his chin. His hair was cut short, parted in the centre and plastered down on his scalp so close that he seemed to be wearing a tight, shiny, black skullcap. His face was round, pink and *extremely* clean. His snub nose was very short – but he still managed to look down it at the scruffy street urchin who stood facing him.

All the Boys thought Billy was rather stuck-up. Wiggins said it was because deep down he was jealous of them. Queenie couldn't see what he had to be jealous of – he was well looked after, while they were often cold and hungry – but Wiggins said it was the special friendship they had with each other, and their freedom to do whatever they liked. Queenie was not convinced. And Billy certainly didn't look jealous now, as he glared at Wiggins.

"Oh, it's you," he sneered. "What d'you want?"

"I'm assisting Mr Holmes on a case," Wiggins

replied with a little smile of triumph. "He wants to see me."

"You sure about that?"

"Course I am. He told me it's a matter of national importance. Now are you gonna let me in?"

"No."

"What d'you mean, no?"

"I mean, Mr Holmes is not in. So he don't need you that bad. He's gone out."

Now it was Billy's turn to smile in triumph. He started to shut the door. Wiggins quickly jammed his foot in the opening, to stop him.

"I'll see Dr Watson, then."

"Can't."

"Why not?"

"'Cos he's gone out as well. Visiting patients." And this time, he did close the door – after he'd stamped on Wiggins's foot.

When he'd stopped hopping around, Wiggins stood still for a moment, wondering what to do next. He decided to take another look at the mysterious iron door, and set off at once for the little alleyway, taking care to keep his eyes open for anything suspicious on the way.

The entrance to the alley was partly blocked by an old beggar man leaning his crooked back against one wall. His face was half hidden by a battered hat with a broad brim, and the tangle of hair that escaped from underneath it was grey and matted, as was his beard. He was selling matches and bootlaces from a tray hung round his neck.

"Wotcha, grandad," Wiggins greeted him cheerfully. "How's business?"

The old man shrugged hopelessly. He looked so dejected that Wiggins dug in his pocket to find a penny. It was his last, but the man obviously needed it more than he did.

"'Fraid I ain't got much," he said, "but here – at least it'll buy you a cup of tea."

"You're a good boy," the old man croaked, sounding grateful.

He held out a shaking hand, but as Wiggins went to place the penny in it, he suddenly found his wrist clamped in a grip of steel.

"A very good boy, Wiggins, my friend!" The voice was that of Sherlock Holmes.

Wiggins gasped, and stared open-mouthed at

the old man. Behind the disguise, he could recognize the familiar piercing eyes of the great detective.

"Mr Ho—" he started to blurt out.

But Mr Holmes cut him short. "Shh! Don't say it!" He looked around, and his voice dropped to a whisper. "There is an old saying: 'Walls have ears.' Never forget that."

"No, sir, Mr ... er... No, sir."

"What are you doing here?"

"I went round your place, but you wasn't there. So I thought I'd take another look at that funny door."

Mr Holmes smiled behind his false beard. "Your instincts are excellent, my young friend. It is indeed a funny door – and a very clever one at that. But I would prefer you not to go near it again for the moment."

"Oh." Wiggins was disappointed, but accepted, as always, that Mr Holmes knew best. "Right, sir. I won't."

"Good. All will be revealed in due course, I promise you. Now, what did you want to see me about?"

"Oh, yes. I wanted to let you know that we've got that house staked out again."

"Good."

"And I've got Shiner keeping watch at Paddington Station."

"Excellent. We shall make a detective of you yet."

"Thank you, sir."

"And? Was there something else you wished to tell me?"

"Yes, sir. There is. I don't know if it means anything…"

"I will be the judge of that. Just give me the facts."

So Wiggins told him about the sinister man he'd seen in the carriage the night before. "He was watching your windows, sir. I'm sure he was."

"Describe him to me."

Wiggins described the man. As he did so, he could sense a growing excitement in the great detective.

Mr Holmes let out a long sigh. "Excellent. You have a good eye for detail, Wiggins. You have drawn a perfect picture of him."

"D'you know him, sir?"

"I believe I do. Was there anything else?"

"Just the one thing. There was something painted on the door of the carriage."

"A monogram, perhaps?"

"An initial: the letter 'M'."

"Moriarty," said Mr Holmes. "So it *was* him."

"Moriarty?" Wiggins asked. "Who's he when he's at home?"

"Professor James Moriarty is the Napoleon of crime, the most dangerous man in London and my deadliest adversary. I believed he had perished during our last encounter, in Switzerland. It would appear that I was mistaken."

Wiggins let out a low whistle. "What's he up to, then?"

"That, my dear Wiggins, is the question. Only when we have discovered what he and his accomplices are plotting can we hope to stop them."

"What d'you want me to do, sir?"

"Go back to your Irregulars, and tell them to keep watching, but tell them to be especially careful. They are to take no risks. I couldn't bear it if I were to cause the death of any of you. Do you understand?"

Wiggins gulped and nodded. This was serious business.

"If you have any new information," Mr Holmes continued, "come back here and report it to me. Otherwise, keep well clear. Now, off you go."

Paddington Station, the London terminus of the Great Western Railway, was busy as usual. Travellers hurried to and fro – those departing anxious not to miss their trains, and those arriving looking out eagerly for friends and relatives meeting them at the platform gates. Porters trundled heavy suitcases and trunks on handcarts and trolleys. Locomotives that had recently arrived stood facing the station concourse, their dark green paintwork streaked with dirt. Smoke rose from their gleaming brass funnels, mingled with escaping steam and climbed lazily up towards the great glass roof. On platform number 1, the famous Cornish Riviera Express stood waiting to depart on its long journey to Penzance, near Land's End – the very tip of the English mainland. The last passengers were climbing into its smart coaches, painted in the railway company's chocolate and cream colours. The last doors slammed shut. The guard was unfurling his green flag, ready to signal the driver to start.

Shiner loved working at the station. He loved the sounds and the smells, the hiss of steam and the shrill blasts of the guards' whistles. He loved the hustle and bustle, and the fact that there was always something going on, and that he was part of it. But most of all, he loved the trains – the engines with their huge iron wheels and their powerful, gleaming piston rods. He loved the noise they made as they started off, the puffs getting louder and faster as they gradually began to pick up speed, straining to haul their heavy loads out of the station.

Shiner had never actually been on a train. But that did not stop him dreaming of being on the footplate of a steam engine, of one day driving a crack express. That was the best job in the whole, wide world, better even than being a famous detective. He would not be a shoeshine boy for ever. One day he would be an engine driver. He looked at the Cornish Riviera Express and sighed deeply.

He was roused from his daydreaming by a fat, elderly man plonking a large foot on his stand so his shoe could be polished. As Shiner looked away from the train, he suddenly caught sight of a broad-brimmed black hat, rising above the heads of the passengers coming out of the gate to platform 4. Deserting his customer, Shiner dropped his brushes and darted across the station concourse, threading his way nimbly through the crowd, until he had a clear view of the streaming passengers. Beneath the hat was the scarred face with the dark moustache, the curly, black fur collar and the heavy coat. The man was carrying a carpet-bag in one hand – and the walking stick with the silver knob in the other. Yes, it was their man. Shiner tailed him as he strode through the station to the cab rank, climbed aboard a hansom cab and was driven away.

"Wiggins! Wiggins! I seen him!" Shiner panted, completely out of breath as he arrived back at HQ. His curly hair clung damply to his thin face, and his dark eyes shone with excitement.

"Whoa, young Shiner!" Wiggins grinned at him from his chair. "Hold your horses! What's up?"

"I just run all the way from Paddington … to tell you."

"To tell me what?"

"The big geezer – he's back!"

"Yeah, I know. Beaver beat you to it. He just saw him getting out of a cab at his house."

"Oh. Did he?" Shiner was deflated.

"Never mind, eh? Can't win 'em all, can you?" Queenie said, giving him a hug of consolation. But he perked up at once. "Bet Beaver don't know where he's been, though, does he?" he said, cocky as ever.

"No. Where?" Wiggins sat up instantly.

"Bristol. He got off the 11.55 express from Bristol Temple Meads."

Rosie was still in position near the alley when Wiggins arrived.

"How's it going?" he asked.

"Not bad. I sold three nosegays and two posies, and…"

"I meant with keeping watch."

"Oh, that," she said, grinning. "Not a dicky bird."

"Nothing?"

"Nobody's gone in. Nobody's come out. Quiet as the grave."

"Very good," he told her in his best commanding-officer tone. "Stick at it."

Wiggins marched purposefully to the alleyway, eager to give Mr Holmes Shiner's latest information. He was sure he would be pleased with it, whatever it might signify. But as he turned the corner he stopped in surprise. The narrow passage was empty. There was no sign of the disguised detective. He had completely disappeared.

A DISGUISED DETECTIVE

"I never moved an inch away from my pitch," Rosie insisted. "If anybody'd come out of this alley I'd have seen 'em."

"I believe you," Wiggins reassured the little flower girl, seeing that she was upset at the thought that she had let him down.

"Anyway," she said defiantly, "what's so special about an old tramp?"

Wiggins looked carefully over his shoulder, then lowered his voice. "That weren't really no old tramp," he whispered. "That was Mr Sherlock Holmes. In disguise."

Rosie's blue eyes opened as wide as carriage lamps. "Well I never!" she exclaimed. Then, sniffing the air, she asked, "'Ere ... can you smell somethin'?"

Wiggins sniffed, then shook his head. "No. Can you?"

"Just a whiff. Sort of like a hospital…"

"You sure?"

"I got a very good sense of smell. Comes of working with flowers. The nicer they smell, the better they sell." She grinned. "Hey, that rhymes! I'm a poet, and I don't know it."

Wiggins grimaced, and scratched his head in bewilderment.

"Wiggins," Rosie asked, "was that old man – Mr Holmes – was he sellin' matches?"

"Yeah."

"Look!" Rosie pointed to the ground.

"What?"

"He's left a trail."

And sure enough, there was a trail of unused matches on the ground, starting at the spot where Mr Holmes had been standing. They followed it along the alley and round the corner. It stopped at the iron door, with its array of locks and bolts. Wiggins stared at the door, thinking hard. Although Mr Holmes had told him not to go near it, he reached out and pushed, testing the locks again. They were as secure as ever.

"Wiggins, I don't like it here," Rosie said, with a shiver. "It's scary."

Wiggins nodded. It felt spooky to him, too, as though invisible eyes were watching them from somewhere. He put a protective arm round Rosie's shoulders and gave her a squeeze. "It's all right," he told her. "I'll take care of you."

She gave him a brave little smile.

"Come on," he said. "Let's get back home. Nothing more we can do here."

"Oh, no. Not you again," Billy the pageboy sniffed at Wiggins. "I already told you – Mr Holmes is not at home."

"I know that. I gotta see Dr Watson."

"Have you got an appointment?"

"Course I ain't."

"Well, then…"

"Just tell him I'm here. It's urgent."

"He's not back yet."

"I'll wait."

"Not on our doorstep. Mrs Hudson wouldn't have it."

"Listen, you toffee-nosed—"

"What's going on here?" a familiar voice interrupted.

Wiggins turned to see Dr Watson standing just behind him, carrying his black doctor's bag.

"This boy wants to see you, Doctor," Billy said in his most officious voice. "He hasn't got an appointment."

"Wiggins!" said the Doctor with a friendly smile. "What is it?"

"I gotta talk to you, Doctor." Wiggins glared at Billy. "In private."

"Ah. You'd better come inside," the Doctor replied, and he led him into the house, past a glowering Billy, who was forced to stand and hold the door open for them.

Dr Watson bent beside the coal fire, warming his hands over the flames.

"Now, Wiggins, my boy," he said. "What is it that is so important it can't be said in front of Billy?"

"It's Mr Holmes, sir," Wiggins replied. "He's disappeared."

"Yes." Dr Watson nodded. "I know."

"You do?" Wiggins was astonished.

"Yes. Nothing unusual, old chap. He's always doing it."

"Disappearing?"

"Absolutely. He dons one of his disguises, and simply drops out of sight."

"No," Wiggins said. "That's not what I meant."

"Amazing transformations. Even fools me sometimes, and that takes a bit of doing, I can tell you."

Wiggins was not so sure about that, but he pressed on. "What I mean is, he's really disappeared. I saw him this morning, dressed up as an old beggar selling matches. But when I went back, he'd gone. The only sign that he'd been there was a trail of matches on the ground."

"I shouldn't worry about it, my boy. He'll show up again when he's good and ready. Why did you want to see him?"

"I had something to tell him."

"Why don't you tell me? And if I see him first I can pass on the message for you."

"Right. This big bloke we've been keeping an eye on, he's back. And he's been to Bristol."

"Bristol?" Dr Watson looked blank. "Are you sure?"

"One of the Boys, young Shiner, saw him getting off the Bristol train."

The doctor still looked blank. "Why should he go to Bristol?"

"I dunno. I thought you might."

"Beats me." He scratched his head. "Now, if Mr Holmes were here…"

"But he ain't, is he?" Wiggins was impatient. "That's what I'm trying to tell you. He ain't just dropped out of sight. I reckon he's been kidnapped!"

Dr Watson smiled and shook his head. "Oh, no," he said calmly. "Mr Holmes is well able to take care of himself. It would take a very good man to kidnap him."

"Or a very bad one," Wiggins retorted. "Like Professor Moriarty!"

Dr Watson looked shocked. "What do you know of Moriarty?" he asked.

"Only what Mr Holmes told me this very morning. That he's his most dangerous enemy."

"*Was*. Moriarty is dead, I'm pleased to say – although I know I shouldn't."

"No he isn't. I've seen him. Right outside your front door."

Dr Watson turned pale.

"Does Mr Holmes know this?"

"Yes, it was him what told me who he was."

"Then that explains where he is. He will be following Moriarty's tracks."

"P'raps Moriarty's been following Mr Holmes's tracks, and now he's trapped him."

"I hardly think that is likely."

"Yeah, but if Mr Holmes didn't even know Moriarty was still alive ... I reckon we should go to the police. Tell Inspector Lestrade."

"Tell him what, exactly? That Mr Holmes has been missing for a couple of hours? And that you think he is being pursued by a dead man?"

"But I know..."

"You know nothing. Haven't you learned anything from Mr Holmes? You must never assume anything, isn't that what he says?"

"Right." Wiggins nodded reluctantly.

"I know his methods. I'm sure he has some

secret plan. We may ruin everything if we interfere."

"We're not gonna do nuffink, then?"

"Anyfink," Dr Watson corrected him. Then corrected himself, "Er, I mean anything. We're not going to do anything. Except wait."

As evening approached, Wiggins sat hunched in his special chair, where he had been all afternoon, thinking hard. To help him concentrate, he had put on the old deerstalker hat he kept especially for such times, and was sucking on the empty pipe.

"Wiggins!" Queenie scolded him. "D'you *have* to make that awful noise?"

The younger Boys, who were sitting around HQ on the floor or on boxes and chairs, tittered as Wiggins sat up and took the pipe from his mouth.

"It's no good," he announced. "I can't just sit here waiting. I gotta do *something*."

"We could go to the coppers," suggested Beaver.

"No. If Dr Watson don't believe us, then Inspector Lestrade won't."

"Course," said Queenie, "Dr Watson *could* be right."

"What d'you mean?"

"Maybe Mr Holmes ain't been kidnapped."

"What about the trail of matches he left?" Rosie piped up.

"You don't *know* he did."

"Yes, I do!" Rosie insisted, getting heated. "I seen 'em."

"Hold your horses!" Wiggins held up a hand to silence Rosie. "Queenie's right. What was it Dr Watson said? 'Never assume anything.' All we can say for sure is that Mr Holmes *might*'ve left them matches as a trail. But he might not've."

"Exactly!" Queenie looked smug. "For all we know, Mr Holmes might've just moved on to somewhere else. And them matches might've just spilled out of his pocket."

"No!" Rosie cried. "He couldn't have moved on."

"He might've been followin' somebody," Gertie chipped in.

"But…" Rosie was close to tears.

Wiggins moved quickly to calm her. "I know,"

he told her. "You'd have seen him. But at least this gives us something to do."

He stood up and clapped his hands for attention. "Listen, everybody," he said. "Here's what we're gonna do. We're gonna split up and go out on the streets, and look everywhere for him and ask everybody we know if they've seen him. Only don't forget, we don't tell nobody who it is we're really looking for. We're looking for an old geezer with a straggly, grey beard and a floppy hat, selling matches and bootlaces. Got it?"

"Got it!" the Boys chorused, glad of the chance to be active. They clambered to their feet and began heading eagerly for the door. Only Sparrow held back.

"What's up, Sparrow?" Wiggins asked him.

"Can't do it," Sparrow replied.

"What's up?" Shiner mocked. "Scared of the dark?"

"No. I gotta go to work."

"Can't the music hall do without you for one night?" asked Wiggins.

"No. They depend on me. I can't let 'em down."

"Quite right," said Queenie. "I'm surprised at you, Arnold Wiggins, for even suggestin' it."

"Sorry."

"'Sides," Sparrow continued, "they got Little Tich toppin' the bill tonight."

"Ah," Wiggins grinned. "Now we're getting the real story. He's your favourite, ain't he?"

"He's the best comic in the whole, wide world. And you know what? He's only about four foot tall. He's even smaller than me! I can't wait to see him."

"Go on, then," Wiggins said, with a smile. "I dare say we'll manage – there's enough of us."

Shiner scowled, and began complaining that it wasn't fair for Sparrow to get out of things. But Queenie grabbed him by the back of the neck and bustled him out the door.

The Boys fanned out into the streets, hunting for any sign of Sherlock Holmes in his disguise. They asked everyone they knew if they had seen the old matchseller: young crossing sweepers, lads holding horses' heads outside hotels, the friendly muffin man who sometimes gave them left-over muffins, messenger boys, flower girls. None of them had seen him.

It was getting dark when Shiner met the old lamplighter, and by that time he was feeling that it was all a waste of time.

"Now then, young Shiner," the old man greeted him, his friendly eyes twinkling. "What you so down in the mouth about?"

"I'm fed up with looking for somebody what ain't there."

"That don't sound very clever," the old man chuckled, stopping beside the next lamppost and lifting the long pole that he carried over one shoulder.

Shiner watched as he poked the brass end with its little flame burning inside it through the bottom of the lamp and lit the gas, as he did every night.

"Who is he?"

"Mr Sher—" Shiner stopped himself just in time. "An old geezer with a grey beard and a floppy hat, selling matches and suchlike."

"Well, why didn't you say so?" the lamplighter said.

"Why? You seen him?"

"Outside Baker Street Station, not a half-hour since. You get a move on, young 'un, he might still be there."

Shiner's face lit up like the streetlamp. This was his chance to show the others. He would be the one to track down the elusive detective. Barely waiting to thank the lamplighter, he dashed off at full speed.

When he arrived at the station a few minutes later, however, at first he could not see the man among the crowds hurrying to catch their trains home. There was a man selling baked potatoes, two or three newsboys shouting the names of their competing papers, and a fat, old woman sitting on a stool among baskets of flowers, singing out, "Violets. Lovely violets!" But no matchseller.

Shiner was about to turn away when he saw the man hobbling out of the station entrance, leaning heavily on a crutch. Shiner let out a little whistle of admiration: it was a really good disguise. He waited until the man had settled himself against a wall to one side of the entrance and put down his tray of matches. Then he sidled up to him, and whispered out of the corner of his mouth, "Psst! Mr 'Olmes!"

The man took no notice of him.

Shiner said it again.

The man looked at him suspiciously. "What d'you want?" he asked harshly.

Shiner was even more impressed: Mr Holmes could obviously disguise his voice as well as his appearance. "It's me – Shiner."

"Clear off!" the man snarled. "Leave me alone."

"It's OK," Shiner whispered. "You don't have to pretend with me. I know who you really are."

The man let out an angry roar, picked up his crutch and hit Shiner with it, knocking him to the ground. Lying in the gutter, Shiner watched as the matchseller made off down the street, surprisingly fast, carrying his crutch in one hand and his tray of matches in the other. The newsboys guffawed at Shiner's plight.

"You all right, son?" the baked-potato seller asked sympathetically.

Shiner nodded.

"What'd you do?"

"I think I made a mistake."

The potato man laughed. "You can say that again, sunshine. That's Basher Brannigan. He's just been in prison for robbery with violence. It don't pay to upset Basher."

Shiner clambered painfully to his feet. "This is stupid," he muttered to himself. "I'm goin' home." And he stomped off towards HQ in a thoroughly bad temper.

THE GREAT GANDINI

It was going to be a special performance at the Imperial Music Hall that night, in aid of charity. Sparrow felt a thrill of excitement as he entered the theatre through the stage door, and caught the familiar smell of greasepaint and the sight of scenery and arc lights. He knew that every artiste on the bill was a star, and that as call boy he would be looking after them – including his personal hero, Little Tich, the biggest, and smallest, star of them all. Usually, Little Tich only played at the smartest theatres in London's West End. But this evening, for one night only, he and the other stars were gracing the stage of the Imperial, which for all its grand name was, in fact, more than a bit shabby.

"Wotcha, me little cock Sparrow," Bert, the

stage doorkeeper, greeted him warmly. "You'll have to be on your toes tonight."

"I will be," Sparrow said happily.

"Can't have nothing go wrong tonight. Not with who we've got coming."

"I know. You ever see him, Bert?"

"Not in the flesh, no."

"They say he's no taller than me."

"What?"

"Little Tich – he's only about four foot tall."

"I was talking about His Royal Highness – the guest of honour."

"Oh, yeah," Sparrow replied. "Him and all."

Bert pushed his peaked uniform cap back, and shook his head indulgently. "What are we going to do with you?" he asked. "Go on, now. And just remember to be on your best behaviour, right?"

Sparrow nodded and skipped off towards the dressing rooms, where the first performers were already putting on their costumes. As top of the bill, Little Tich would be on stage last, so he would not be arriving at the theatre until after the interval. But there was plenty to keep

Sparrow busy until then. He changed quickly into the jacket the manager made him wear – it was very like Billy's uniform, with shiny brass buttons up the front – and went to see if anyone needed anything.

In the first dressing room, a trio of acrobats were limbering up, bending and stretching so far that it made Sparrow's arms and legs ache just looking at them.

The leader called out to him, and asked him to fetch a plate of ham sandwiches from the bar. "A big plateful," he stressed. "Got to keep our strength up in this business, you know!"

In the next room, a fat lady singer cleared her throat and trilled a few scales. "Oh dear, oh dear," she moaned. "Don't I sound terrible? I need a gargle."

Sparrow secretly agreed with her, and doubted that gargling would improve things. Nevertheless, he took the shilling she gave him to buy her "a large gin and polly" from the bar. It would ease her poor throat, she told him confidentially.

A cockney comic, dressed as a pearly king with thousands of shiny pearl buttons sewn all over his suit, was passing by at that moment. "Need a spot of the old lubrication, Nellie?" he asked, with a cheeky grin. Turning away, he gave Sparrow a huge wink and added quietly, "Like putting oil on a squeaky gate, eh, son?"

Sparrow only just managed not to laugh out loud, before hurrying off to the bar through the pass door that led from backstage to the "front of house". The orchestra was tuning up, ready to start playing. In the gilded auditorium, the faded, red plush seats were filling with people wearing evening dress. Way up above in the top-most gallery – known as "the gods" – poorer people were packing on to the hard benches, laughing and joking and leaning forward to catch a glimpse of the "nobs" below them. The whole theatre was filled with an expectant buzz. Sparrow breathed in the atmosphere, looked around at the happy faces and decided that he was in the most exciting place in the entire universe.

The first half of the programme went very well. The audience laughed at the cockney comic's

jokes, gasped at the twists and turns of the acrobats, marvelled at the skill of the jugglers, and
even listened enraptured to the fat lady singer –
to Sparrow's surprise, the "lubrication" seemed
to have worked wonders on her voice. As the
applause died away, the theatre manager strode
on to the stage to announce the final act before
the interval.

"Your Royal Highness," he proclaimed. "My
lords, ladies and gentlemen! It is my proud
privilege to present to you an artiste we have
brought over, at *enormous* expense to the
management, all the way from Milano in sunny
Italy. A man who has performed for the crowned
heads of Europe and the world. Ladies and
gentlemen, I give you the magician magnificent,
escapologist extraordinaire, the one and only –
the Great Gandini!"

The Great Gandini was a rather oily, middle-
aged man, whose twirly, black moustache turned
up at each end into sharp, waxed points. He was
slim but well muscled, and wore a rather shiny
dress suit, complete with white bow tie and tail-
coat. He was assisted by an attractive young

woman, with wavy, black hair, wearing a tight-fitting dress of scarlet satin. Because it was the interval next, and he did not have to call any more artistes, Sparrow was able to stand in the "wings" at the side of the stage and watch as the magician performed a series of tricks, each more amazing than the last. He made doves appear and rabbits disappear. He produced coins and eggs from people's ears. He stole people's watches and produced them in other people's pockets. He presented a lady with a large bouquet of real flowers that he had conjured out of a small pocket handkerchief. And all the time, he kept up a continuous patter, addressing the audience in a heavy Italian accent, with almost every word seeming to end in "o" or "a".

Sparrow was enthralled by it all. But it was the Great Gandini's final trick that really grabbed his attention. With the help of a volunteer from the audience, the assistant fastened the magician's wrists with handcuffs and bound his arms and legs with chains. She secured these with strong padlocks, which she asked the volunteer to check. Then a large wooden chest was wheeled on to the stage, and also checked carefully to confirm that it was solid. The assistant opened the hinged lid, the escapologist climbed inside and the lid was closed and fastened with a heavy iron bolt and another padlock, the key to which was given to the volunteer to hold. A black curtain with a silver moon and stars sewn onto it descended from the "flies" above the stage, to hide the locked chest from the audience. Standing in front of the black curtain with the volunteer, the assistant started a large clock, which ticked very loudly, and the drummer in the orchestra began playing a drum roll.

Watching, fascinated, from the wings, Sparrow heard the rattle and clank of chains from inside the chest. Then, to his amazement, the lid of the chest opened and the Great Gandini climbed out, free of chains and handcuffs. He closed the lid again, then pushed through the curtain to be greeted by wild applause. When the curtain was raised once more, the volunteer checked that the chest was still fastened. He took the key and undid the padlock, and found the chains and handcuffs lying in the empty chest.

Sparrow could hardly believe what he had seen. All day he had been puzzling over the mystery of the iron door. Could this be the answer? During the interval, when Gandini had retired to his dressing room to pack up the rest of his equipment, Sparrow crept over to the chest, which had been pushed into a corner, ready to be dismantled and taken away. Having seen how the trick had been done, he had a pretty good idea what he was looking for, and it did not take him long to find it. He was just lifting the lid when he heard an angry roar behind him.

"Hey! What d'you think you're doin'?" Gandini was so furious his face was livid. In fact, he was so angry he had quite forgotten he was supposed to be Italian, and was speaking in a broad north-country English accent.

"I … nothin'. Nothin'. Honest," Sparrow stammered, afraid of the angry magician and confused by his sudden change of nationality.

"You're messing wi' my things!"

"I'm sorry, Mr Gandini, sir. I ain't done no harm."

"No harm? No harm? What's that got to do wi' it, you little tike?"

"What's going on here? Is this personage causing you annoyance, Signor Gandini?" It was the theatre manager, Mr Trump. He looked at Sparrow accusingly.

"He was messing wi' my stuff," Gandini snarled. He swung back to Sparrow. "You never, never, touch a magician's props. Don't you know that's the cardinal rule of this business?"

"What's that mean?" asked Sparrow.

"It means a rule that must be obeyed," Mr Trump snapped.

"I… I'm sorry, sir. I didn't mean to… Only, you see…"

The manager silenced him with a wave of his hand, and spoke to Gandini again. "Pray accept my most compunctious apologies," he grovelled.

"What sort of staff do you employ here?" Gandini demanded.

"He's regrettably inexperienced," the manager continued. "He doesn't know any better."

"Well it's time he learnt," Gandini spat.

"I want him out of here!"

"Yes. Of course."

"Now!"

Mr Trump turned to Sparrow again. "You're fired!"

Sparrow was close to tears. "No. Please," he begged. "I can explain. It's important."

"Well?" The manager loomed over him. "It had better be good."

"You see, there's this door, and..." Sparrow stopped as he realized he wasn't supposed to say anything.

"I'm waiting."

"Who put you up to this?" asked Gandini.

"I'm sorry. I can't tell you. It's a secret."

"I'll bet it is," Gandini snorted. He turned back to the manager. "The secrets are mine. And he was trying to steal them."

"No, I weren't. Honest. Give me another chance. I won't do it again, I promise."

"Get out of here," the manager growled. "And don't come back."

"Oh, please... Can't I just stay and see Little Tich?"

"No. And divest yourself of that garment before you depart."

Heartbroken, Sparrow slipped out of the call boy's jacket and dragged himself to the door. His dreams were shattered. As he left, a hansom cab drew up outside the stage door and a figure hopped nimbly out. It was Little Tich. Sparrow watched as the tiny comedian paused to exchange greetings with Bert, before disappearing into the theatre. Then he turned away and trudged miserably home.

TRAPPED!

Back at HQ, Sparrow flung himself down on his bed, weeping miserably. The only other Boy at home was Shiner, who was still upset by his encounter with Basher Brannigan and did not want to hear Sparrow's troubles. After a few minutes, however, his curiosity got the better of him, and he couldn't resist asking what was the matter.

"Nothin'," Sparrow replied, burying his face in his mattress so that Shiner wouldn't see his tears.

"Don't look like nothin' to me," Shiner said, not unkindly.

"Nothin's the matter. I'm all right."

"What you cryin' for, then?"

"I ain't," Sparrow insisted, sniffing loudly.

"And what you doin' here?" Shiner went on.

"I thought you was s'posed to be at the theatre?"

That started Sparrow off again. "I was," he sobbed. "I got the sack."

"What they do that for?" Shiner asked indignantly. "I thought they liked you."

"The Great Gandini don't. It was him what got me chucked out."

"The great what? Who's he when he's at home?"

"Gandini – magician magnificent, escapologist extraordinaire."

"Blimey! That's a bit of a mouthful, ain't it? What's it mean? Esca-what-you-call-it?"

"Escapologist. Means he escapes."

"Like from prison, you mean? He's an escaped convict?"

"No," Sparrow replied scornfully. "He gets out of handcuffs and chains and locked boxes and things."

"Oh." Shiner was disappointed. An escaped criminal would have been exciting. "So what happened?"

"He caught me lookin' at his props."

"His what?"

"Props. Things what artistes use on stage, in their acts."

"To prop 'em up, so they don't fall down?" Shiner grinned at the picture this conjured up in his mind.

"No, stupid. It's short for 'properties'."

"And what's that mean?"

"How should I know? It's just what they're called. You gonna listen now? This is important."

Sparrow sat up. He had stopped crying as he remembered what he had discovered. His eyes, though still red, were bright with excitement as he described Gandini's escape from the locked chest. To his surprise, however, Shiner was not impressed.

"You mean it was all a trick?" he asked.

Sparrow sighed impatiently. "Course it was a trick, you dummy!" he almost shouted at Shiner. "It's all a trick. He ain't even Italian, he just pretends to be."

"Who you callin' a dummy?" Shiner snapped, mightily offended.

"You, of course," Sparrow snapped back. "Can't you see what I'm tellin' you?"

"What?"

"I know how it works!" Sparrow crowed triumphantly.

Shiner stared at him dully. "What good's that?" he asked. "All that's done is get you the sack."

Sparrow let out a cry of exasperation and beat one hand against his forehead. "I'm talkin' about the mystery door, you dope. I reckon it works just like Gandini's trick chest. I know how to open it!" And he went on to describe exactly how the trick chest worked.

Shiner found it hard to understand – which was not really surprising, since Sparrow's explanation was rather garbled. But, being Shiner, there was no way he would admit this. "Garn!" he scoffed. "You're makin' it all up."

"I ain't!"

"You're makin' it all up, so you can look clever."

"You callin' me a fibber?"

"We all know how you likes tellin' tall tales."

This was perfectly true: Sparrow did like a good story, and he was not above spicing up his tales to make them more exciting. But this time he did not need to, and he was very upset when Shiner refused to believe him. The disagreement became a quarrel and the quarrel became more and more heated, until Sparrow could stand it no longer and stormed out into the night.

"I'll show you!" he hurled back over his shoulder. "You'll be sorry!"

Shiner shrugged, and went to bed. Before long he was fast asleep.

The night seemed darker than usual as Sparrow made his way along the street. The shadows between the pools of light cast by the gas lamps were deep black. Anyone, or anything, could be hiding in them. But Sparrow was a boy with a mission. He swallowed hard and hurried on, until he reached the entrance of the alleyway leading to the iron door. His eyes were becoming used to the dim light, but the alley itself was even darker and gloomier than the street. He wished he had had the sense to bring the bull's-eye lantern that Wiggins kept at HQ, but he couldn't go back for it now.

Sparrow took a deep breath and started walking

down the alley, feeling his way cautiously. But just before he reached the bend where it turned to the right, he heard a sound from the alleyway ahead of him, the dull clang of the metal door being closed. It was followed by voices, speaking very low. Sparrow looked around desperately, but there was nowhere to hide. Suddenly the men came into view round the corner, lighting their way with a bull's-eye lantern of their own. There were two of them – one middle-aged, the other much younger. Both were short and wiry, and both wore dark suits, flat cloth caps and white silk scarves knotted around their necks.

The light picked up Sparrow as he turned to run.

"Hey, you!" the older man called, and then stopped. "Ah, sure and it's only a kid."

"Yeah," his companion replied. "Just some little ragamuffin."

"Get outta here, kid!" the first man shouted. "And don't come back. There's nuttin' for youse down here."

The voices sounded Irish, or American – Sparrow was not sure which. But he didn't stay to find out. Once in the street, he dived into the first doorway for cover. From there, he watched the two men emerge from the alley and look furtively around before moving off.

Now Sparrow was faced with a quandary: should he follow the men and find out where they were going? Or should he take advantage of the fact that they had left, and try his luck with the door? He was eager to test the lock, but he might learn more of what they were up to if he followed them. He decided to follow them, dodging from doorway to doorway so as not to be seen.

He did not have far to go. After only a few hundred yards, they stopped and entered a pub, and when Sparrow peeped through the window he saw the two men buying large glasses of ale at the bar and then settling themselves down in a corner. They looked as though they intended to stay there for some time. Sparrow thought fast. Now was his chance. He turned and hurried back to the alley.

It was so dark at the far end of the alley, cut off from even the tiniest glimmer of light from the street, that Sparrow only found the door by feeling for it with his arms stretched out like a blind man. Once again, he cursed himself for not thinking to bring a lantern. He moved his hands over the cold, rough surface of the door, trying to make out the padlock and bolts, and the hinges. It was impossible, and he could have cried with frustration. But then he felt something scrunch under his feet, and as he moved there was a sharp fizzing sound, and a familiar smell. Could it be? Hardly daring to hope, Sparrow bent down and felt along the ground. Yes! It could. Matches! The matches that Sherlock Holmes had dropped! He gathered a handful, stood up and struck one against the rough wall. It burst into flame, allowing him to see the door quite clearly.

Sparrow needed three matches before he finally managed to work out how the lock worked, trying to remember exactly what he had seen at the theatre. But suddenly he had done it. Sparrow swung the door open, then nervously stepped inside.

He found himself in a large storeroom, dimly

lit by two oil lamps that the men had left burning but turned down low. Along the far wall, there was a workbench scattered with tools and odd pieces of equipment. To one side stood two camp beds, covered with rumpled blankets, showing they had been slept in, and a bulging carpet-bag. A square kitchen table was littered with used mugs, glasses, bottles, plates and cutlery. There were two wooden packing cases pushed against the opposite wall, one large and the other smaller. A large cabin trunk with a rounded lid stood on its end in the centre of the room, looking as though it was ready for a journey.

Sparrow did not know what he was searching for, but he poked around the room, hoping to spot a clue. He wished Wiggins were there – he would know exactly what to look for. Perhaps whatever was in the packing cases would give him an idea. But when he lifted the lid of the first one, it turned out to be empty, apart from a heap of wood shavings. The other contained a mixture of odds and ends, including a box filled with cardboard tubes and coils of what looked like thick string. Sparrow moved on to the cabin trunk, which had labels pasted on it picturing an ocean liner and the name "White Star Line". This was more like it. Sparrow began to examine the trunk more carefully. Curiously, it had a number of small holes drilled in the lid.

Suddenly he heard something that made him freeze with fright. It was the sound of breathing. Steady breathing, like someone in a deep sleep. And it was coming from inside the trunk. With trembling fingers, Sparrow started to unfasten the big brass catch to open the lid, when he heard something that scared him even more: the sound of the iron door opening. He looked around desperately. Where could he hide? Remembering the wooden packing cases, Sparrow rushed across the room, pulled open the larger one and climbed in, sliding the lid over the top of him.

Sparrow had barely closed the lid when he heard someone entering the room. The gaps between the boards of the packing case were just wide enough to let air in, but too small to let him see out. It sounded as though there was only one person, moving quietly about. Sparrow thought he heard the catch on the trunk being snapped undone, followed by a slight creak that could have been the lid opening. And then a low, sinister chuckle, so evil it made his skin prickle. A moment later, he heard the unmistakable sound of a cork being pulled out of a bottle, and a sickly sweet smell reached his nostrils, making him feel quite woozy. He fought off the feeling. If he should go to sleep, he might miss something – or he might snore and give himself away, which would be even worse.

The unseen man laughed again. "Enjoy your sleep, my friend," Sparrow heard him murmur. "It will be your last."

Sparrow heard the trunk being closed, and then, to his horror, he heard the man's footsteps approaching his packing case. Sparrow waited in terror for the lid to be opened. His heart was thumping so loudly he was sure it would give him away. But instead of opening the packing case, the man sat down on it, using it as a seat.

After that, there was silence for what seemed to Sparrow like a very long time. Eventually, however, he heard the scraping of the bolts on the iron door, and then the voices of the two men. They stopped abruptly.

"Professor!" one of the men said nervously. "You're early."

The response came as a venomous hiss. "Where have you been?"

"Er, we went to get refreshments," the man stammered.

"That's right," the second man added. "We needed refreshments, your honour."

"You left him alone!"

"Sure, and he's not goin' nowheres," the first man replied.

The man they had called Professor spoke with cold anger. "You fools!" he spat. "Do you not realize with whom you are dealing?"

"Now then, Professor," the second man said, soothingly. "There's no harm done, to be sure. He's still here, is he not? And everything's ready."

"Everything?" the Professor asked.

"Everything. All prepared and ready to go for our meeting with the widow. Come see for yourself."

The packing case creaked as the Professor stood up. The three men moved away to the far corner of the room, and Sparrow found it hard to hear what they were saying, as they talked to each other in low voices. He could only catch the occasional word or phrase, as the Professor gave what were obviously instructions to the two men. There was something about a train, and then a boat. Sparrow could not make out exactly what, but he did hear him say, quite clearly, "over the water".

Straining to listen, Sparrow tried to twist himself round to press one ear against the side of the case. As he did so, the muscles of his left leg, which was screwed up beneath him, suddenly cramped. The pain was excruciating. He wanted to scream, to straighten up and stretch the leg, but somehow he managed to control himself, clenching his teeth really hard and holding his breath until the cramp gradually eased. The men were still talking. Sparrow did not know how much he had missed, but he heard one of them say something about a grand opening going with a bang, which made the other men chortle. Then he heard the Professor's voice, quiet but full of menace, saying "utter disgrace … the end of Mr Sherlock Holmes". This was followed by a particularly nasty laugh.

After a short pause, the Professor announced, "It's time to go. Anything you need, take it now. There'll be no coming back to this place after tomorrow."

Sparrow heard the noise of things being dragged across the floor. The packing case shook, as something was dumped on top of it. There was a dull rumble, as a heavy weight was wheeled away. And then the iron door clanged shut and all was quiet.

In the silence, Sparrow could hear a loud ticking, like a clock, just above his head. He rubbed the leg that had had cramp, which was still sore. He needed to stand up and stretch it, before the cramp came back again. But even more than that, he needed to get out and run to find Wiggins and the others, to tell them what he'd heard.

Sparrow pushed on the lid. It wouldn't open. He tried again. It was impossible. Whatever had been put on top of the packing case was too heavy. The ticking above his head seemed to get louder and louder. He was trapped – and nobody knew where he was.

A Bomb in a Box

The Great Gandini towered over Sparrow, his face contorted in fury. "I'll teach you to keep your nose out of my business," he snarled. He wrapped a chain round the helpless boy, pinioning his arms tightly to his side, and fastened it with a huge padlock. Sparrow suddenly noticed that the magician had grown taller, and was wearing a wide-brimmed black hat and a heavy coat with a curly fur collar. He was now, Sparrow realized, the big man they had been trailing earlier. Another man stood behind him, laughing coldly. Sparrow could not see his face, but he knew that it was the evil Professor.

"Drop him down the well," the Professor hissed. "They'll never find him there."

Then Sparrow saw a black hole in front of

him, so deep it seemed to have no bottom. The two men from the storeroom appeared from the shadows, seized Sparrow and started to drag him towards the hole...

And then Sparrow woke up, trembling from his bad dream. He was almost relieved to find he was still inside the packing case. It was pitch black and totally silent, and he was very frightened. But he had been so tired after all the events of the day that he had fallen asleep. Sparrow had no idea how long he had slept, but the empty feeling in his stomach suggested it had been some time. He would still have been sleeping, but something had disturbed him. He became aware that someone was moving around the room.

Suddenly alert, Sparrow listened hard. Was it the Professor back again? Or the big man? What should he do? If he called out, he might be in even greater danger, but at least he would be rescued from the packing case. It was a difficult decision. He held his breath in fear. Then someone called out "Ow!" and someone else made a shushing noise.

"Sorry," the first voice said. "I hurt my toe."

Sparrow could hardly believe his ears. It was Beaver!

"Oi!" he shouted, as loudly as he could.

There was a scream, and a bump as something was knocked over.

"There's somebody here!" That was Queenie's voice.

"Can't see nobody," came Gertie's voice. "Must be invisible."

"It's a ghost!" That was Rosie.

"No, it ain't!" Sparrow shouted. "It's me!"

"Sparrow?" Wiggins called.

"Yeah! Get me out of here!"

"Where are you?"

"Over here! In the big box!"

A flicker of light penetrated a crack in the packing case, as Wiggins shone his lantern over it.

"What's he doin' in there?" Shiner asked.

Beaver lifted off the smaller packing case, which was trapping Sparrow in his hiding place. Wiggins opened the lid, and a very grateful Sparrow popped up like a jack-in-the-box, a grin on his face that seemed to stretch from one ear to the other.

"Am I pleased to see you lot!" he exclaimed happily.

In the light of the lantern, the others grinned back at him – all except Beaver, who was standing holding the smaller packing case and looking puzzled.

"What's that ticking noise?" he asked.

Sparrow suddenly realized what he had been sleeping with. "It's a bomb!" he yelled. "There's a bomb in there!"

Beaver froze. So did all the others.

"Can't you hear it?" asked Sparrow.

Wiggins nodded, signalled to the others to stand back, and gingerly opened the lid. Inside was an assortment of bottles and boxes, books and bags, and a large brass alarm clock with two bells on top, ticking merrily. As Wiggins picked it up, the alarm went off with a deafening clangour. Rosie and Gertie screamed. Shiner, Queenie and Beaver dived for cover. Sparrow dropped back into his packing case.

Wiggins laughed. "There's your bomb!" he said, switching off the alarm.

Sparrow emerged from the packing case again,

looking sheepish. "Well, how was I to know? It was tickin'."

"Sure and isn't that what clocks do?" Gertie teased.

"Never you mind, Sparrow," Queenie comforted him, helping him out of the case and brushing wood shavings from his hair and clothes. "You was very brave, comin' here on your own."

"Very stupid, more like," said Wiggins sternly.

"I wanted to know if the door worked like I thought," Sparrow replied.

"And it did," Wiggins continued. "What d'you think would have happened if we hadn't found you?"

"Dunno." Sparrow shrugged, trying not to show how frightened he had been. "You took your time gettin' here, didn't you?"

"We didn't know where you was," Beaver said defensively.

"If it hadn't been for Shiner, we'd never have known," Queenie added. "You should say thank you to him."

Sparrow grunted at Shiner, and then said grudgingly, "Ta. Ta very much."

"S'all right," Shiner said, gloating slightly.

"We never even knew you wasn't there," said Beaver, "when we got back to HQ."

"Shiner was asleep," Rosie explained. "So he didn't tell us you'd gone out. We thought you was still at the theatre."

"We all went to bed," Gertie said, stifling a yawn at the thought of sleep.

"How d'you find out, then?"

"Queenie stayed up, waitin' for you to come home," Beaver told him. "Like she always does."

Queenie gave a little cough, to cover her embarrassment. "I weren't sleepy," she said.

"And when you hadn't come back by one o'clock, she started worryin'."

"Like she always does," Shiner chipped in, with a wicked grin.

"That's quite enough of that, my lad," Queenie scolded him. She went on to say how she had woken up Shiner, to ask him if he had seen Sparrow.

"And I told her how you'd got the sack," Shiner said gleefully. "And all that stuff you was tellin' me about the trick locks and fake hinges and the door openin' back to front and everythin'."

"Yeah, what you didn't believe," Sparrow retorted.

"It didn't make much sense to *me* at first," said Wiggins. "Particularly the way Shiner told it. But I managed to work it out. And here we are."

"Lucky for you," Queenie said. "What's been goin' on? Who put you in there?"

"Nobody," Sparrow said. "I was hidin'. There was these two geezers—"

"Two geezers?" Shiner interrupted. "What if they come back? Let's get out of here!"

"No, they won't," Sparrow said. "When they left, they said they wasn't never coming back no more."

"Well in that case," said Wiggins, "let's have a bit more light on the scene." He struck a match and lit the two oil lamps. "There, that's better. Now we can see what we're doing."

They all looked around. Sparrow let out a yelp.

"Oh, it's gone!"

"What's gone?" Wiggins asked.

"The trunk. A big cabin trunk, it was. Stood right there. And there was somebody shut inside it."

"Who?"

"Dunno." I could hear him breathin', but I didn't see him—"

He stopped as the truth suddenly dawned.

"I reckon it was Mr Holmes!"

There was a loud gasp from all the Boys.

"Nah," Shiner piped up. "Not Mr Holmes. It couldn't have been."

"Oh, yes, it could," Beaver said, holding up something he had found in the smaller packing case. At first sight, it looked like some sort of small, furry animal, but when Beaver put it up to his chin, the others could see what it was.

"It's a false beard!" Gertie exclaimed. "It don't suit you at all."

"The false beard Mr Holmes was wearing!" said Wiggins.

"And look," Beaver went on. He lifted a tray of matchboxes and an old, floppy hat out of the packing case. "The rest of his disguise. He *was* here."

"And now they've took him away," Sparrow cried.

"Where to?"

"Dunno. They never said." Sparrow was on

the verge of tears.

"Whoa! Steady on, now!" Wiggins squeezed Sparrow's shoulder. "It's not your fault."

"Wiggins is right," Beaver reassured him. "Weren't nothin' you could do about it."

Wiggins tipped his hat back on his head and looked thoughtful. "Now then," he told Sparrow. "I want you to take it slowly and try to tell me everything you saw and heard."

"And smelt," Rosie chipped in.

"Smelt?" Wiggins asked, puzzled.

"Yeah. It's here again – that same smell as before."

Wiggins and the others all sniffed the air, curiously.

"You're right, Rosie," he said. "It is."

Sparrow nodded vigorously. "Yeah!" he exclaimed. "There *was* a smell. Nearly knocked me out, it did. I heard this other geezer pull a cork out of a bottle…"

"Other geezer?" Wiggins asked.

"Oh, yeah. I didn't tell you yet, did I? There was this other bloke, like the boss. They called him 'Perfesser'."

Wiggins's eyes narrowed. "Professor? Ha!" He nodded seriously, in his best Sherlock Holmes manner. "Moriarty. The game's afoot!"

The others looked baffled.

"What game?" Gertie asked.

"Didn't you hear? Football," Shiner replied.

"No, no," Wiggins said impatiently. "It's what Mr Holmes says when things start to hot up."

"What if they come back?" Queenie asked, nervously.

"They won't," said Wiggins.

"You don't know where they've gone. It might not be far."

"No," Sparrow said, remembering. "This Perfesser geezer, he told the others to take everythin' they needed, 'cos they wouldn't be comin' back here. He said they could leave the rest, 'cos it wouldn't matter after tomorrow."

Wiggins nodded again. "That means whatever they're gonna do, they're gonna do tomorrow. So we ain't got much time to find out what it is and put a stop to it."

"And rescue Mr Holmes," Queenie reminded him.

"Yes, yes, of course. Now then, young Sparrow, just you sit down here and tell us everything you can remember."

So Sparrow did, trying to recall every word the Professor had said. It wasn't easy, because he hadn't heard very clearly, and most of what he had heard hadn't made much sense. But he did his best, and Wiggins listened hard, his forehead furrowed and his eyes half closed in concentration.

When Sparrow had finished, Wiggins still sat deep in thought, murmuring the key words to himself. Then he stood up and began pacing the room, stopping every now and then to poke about for anything that might give him a clue. Among the tools scattered on the workbench he found a piece of cotton wool, about the size of his hand. He picked it up, sniffed at it, then called Rosie over.

"That it?" he asked her.

She raised the cotton wool to her nose, but quickly lowered it again, blinking rapidly as she nodded. "Cor," she said, coughing. "Fair makes your eyes water, don't it? What is it?"

"I reckon that's chloroform," Wiggins informed her. "What they use in the hospital to put you to sleep."

"They must have used that on Mr Holmes!" Sparrow cried.

"Yeah, I 'spect that's how they captured him," Gertie agreed, her eyes wide.

"They'd never have took him prisoner no other way," Beaver added. "Not Mr Holmes."

Wiggins continued to pace to and fro, deeply puzzled. "You're right," he muttered. "But why put him to sleep? If they wanted to do him in, why didn't they just bash him over the head?"

"If we knew where they'd took him, we might be able to tell what they're gonna do," Queenie suggested helpfully.

"Bristol!" Shiner shouted. "Don't you remember? That big bloke got off the Bristol Express."

"Well done, Shiner," Queenie congratulated him. "But, what's at Bristol?"

"Ships," said Gertie. "That's where me dad and me landed when we come over from Ireland! They got docks right in the middle of the city."

"Yeah!" Sparrow called out excitedly. "I remember now, I heard the Perfesser say somethin' about 'over the water' and 'on the boat'."

"Now we're gettin' somewhere," Beaver said.

Wiggins stopped pacing and turned back to Sparrow. "But we still don't know what they're plotting. Think hard, now. Is there anything else they said?"

Sparrow screwed up his face with the effort of remembering. "There was somethin' about meetin' a widow," he said. "And a train…"

"Yes, yes," Wiggins encouraged him. "Go on."

"P'raps there's somethin' in that box what might give us a clue," Beaver joined in. "Or at least help Sparrow to remember." He started unpacking the contents of the smaller packing case and laying everything out on the floor.

Sparrow looked at each item and shook his head. When everything was laid out, he looked puzzled. "There's somethin' missin'," he said.

"What?" Wiggins asked him.

"Dunno. When I looked in that box, there weren't all this stuff. They must have put this lot in when they was clearin' up. But there was somethin' else..." Suddenly his face cleared. "I know. There was a bundle of sort of cardboard tubes, all tied together."

"How big? How big were the tubes?" Wiggins asked.

"Oh, 'bout an inch across, and 'bout this long." He held his hands about nine inches apart. "I thought they might have had cigars in 'em, but they was a bit too big. Then I thought p'raps they was fireworks, but they was wrapped very plain. And there was some cord with 'em, like wick for an oil lamp."

"Like this?" Wiggins picked up a short piece of cord.

"Yeah, that's it. Only there was a lot more. All coiled up, it was."

Wiggins looked very serious. He fingered the cord and sniffed at it, examining it carefully. Then he reached for a match, struck it, and held it against the end of the cord. The cord caught alight. It did not flame, but fizzed and sparked. The Boys watched, fascinated, as it burned down. Wiggins licked his thumb and forefinger and pinched out the spark.

"That ain't lamp wick," he announced solemnly. "That's a fuse. And them cardboard tubes you saw, Sparrow, they wasn't fireworks. They was sticks of dynamite."

Six pale faces stared at him, open-mouthed and wide-eyed.

"*That's* your bomb," he told them. "And wherever them villains have gone, they've took it with 'em."

THREE HALVES TO WINDSOR

The Boys now knew that the Professor and his two henchmen were going to blow up something or somebody. But who or what, where and when remained a mystery. Wiggins wondered what Mr Holmes would do in this situation. He'd probably get his violin out, he thought, and start playing. Mercifully, Wiggins had no violin, so the rest of the Boys were spared that. In the storeroom he didn't have his chair either, or his pipe, or even his deerstalker hat, to help him think. Instead, he paced the floor, holding the piece of charred fuse in his hand. And as he paced, he muttered to himself, going over and over everything they had discovered so far, trying to work out what the villains were up to.

The other Boys watched and waited quietly, taking care not to disturb him.

But after several minutes Wiggins was no nearer to finding an answer. He turned back to Sparrow. "Let's go over it all again," he said. "Are you sure you've remembered everything you heard?"

"Yeah, I'm sure. They was goin' on about the widow, and a train and somethin' about over the water…"

"They're gonna kill somebody," Queenie said, "and when they do, his wife will be a widow. Right?"

"Well, they couldn't be talkin' about Mr Holmes, then," Beaver replied. "He ain't married."

"No, he ain't," Wiggins agreed. "It's gotta be somebody else."

Sparrow felt a twinge in his leg. He stood up to rub his sore calf muscle, and as he did, the pain reminded him of the cramp he'd had when he was inside the packing case, and what he'd heard the men saying then. "Hang on," he cried excitedly. "There *was* somethin' else. I just remembered."

Wiggins stopped pacing. "Yes?" he asked.

"What was it, now? Oh, yes, I got it. They said 'That'll make the grand openin' go with a bang!' and then they laughed."

"Well, that's easy enough," Queenie said. "A bomb makes a bang, don't it?"

Wiggins held up his hand. "Never mind the bomb," he said. "What about the rest of it? The grand opening? That's gotta be a clue."

"It would be if we knew what was bein' opened," Beaver said, gloomily.

There was a moment of silence as they all pondered this.

Then Shiner piped up. "The Queen's openin' a new railway station today," he said. "It's a present to her from the Great Western, for her jubilee."

"Well, why didn't you say before?" Wiggins asked impatiently.

"'Cos it ain't at Bristol, it's at Windsor. Right by her castle."

The others sighed with disappointment. But Wiggins's face lit up.

"That's it!" he shouted, very excited. "They was

talking about the Queen! *She's* the widow. That's what people call her: 'the Widow at Windsor'."

"Oh, my oath!" Queenie exclaimed. "They're gonna blow up the Queen!"

"And Mr Holmes with her," Rosie added, deeply shocked, like all the Boys.

They were speechless for a moment, before Shiner broke the silence.

"But what about Bristol?" he asked.

"P'raps they're gonna escape that way," Gertie suggested. "Catch the train to Bristol and then a ship over the water to Ireland or America or somewhere."

Wiggins's forehead furrowed as he tried to solve the riddle. Suddenly his face cleared as he thought of the answer. "Bristol ain't got nothing to do with it!" he cried.

"But what about the big man and the train?" Beaver asked.

Wiggins turned to Shiner. "How d'you get to Windsor by train?" he demanded.

"Paddington to Slough, then change onto the special branch line to Windsor," Shiner answered promptly.

"Right. And where do the trains from Bristol stop on the way back to London?"

"Bath, and Swindon, and Reading and… And Slough!" Shiner yelled, excited at seeing the light. "Last stop for the Express – Slough!"

"Precisely, my dear Shiner," Wiggins replied, sounding exactly like Mr Holmes. "Our man never went to Bristol. He went to Windsor – and he got on the Bristol to London train at Slough!"

The other Boys gazed at Wiggins in admiration.

"Brilliant!" Beaver told him. "That settles it."

"Yeah, but what we gonna do about it?" Queenie asked.

"We're gonna stop it, of course," said Wiggins.

"How?"

"Dunno yet. But I'll think of something." He turned to Shiner again. "Now then, when's this grand opening of yours?"

"Tomorrow mornin' sometime."

Wiggins pulled his watch from his pocket and consulted it. "It's tomorrow morning already," he announced. "Come on, everybody. We got no time to lose."

Queenie grabbed him by the sleeve as he

headed for the door. "Hang on!" she said. "Where we goin', and what's the plan?"

"Plan. Right. The plan..." Wiggins was transformed into the commander briefing his troops. "Right. Listen, everybody, this is what we're gonna do: we're gonna split into two parties – Queenie, Beaver and Rosie, I want you to go to Baker Street, wake up Dr Watson and tell him what's going on."

"Why us?" Queenie demanded.

"'Cos he'll believe you three. And just in case he don't – here, take these to show him." He picked up Mr Holmes's floppy hat, wig and false beard, and handed them to her.

"Right," she said, tucking them away in the pocket of her pinafore. "Don't worry – I'll make him believe us."

"That's the stuff. Then get him to take you to Inspector Lestrade at Scotland Yard. Lestrade will listen to him."

"What're *you* gonna do?" Beaver wanted to know, upset at the thought that he might be missing out on the most exciting part of the action.

"The rest of us – that's Shiner, Sparrow, Gertie

and me – are going to Windsor. We'll need Inspector Lestrade to telegraph the coppers there, to warn 'em. That's real important, Beaver. Matter of fact, it's vital. Life and death. Right?"

"Right. You can rely on us."

Queenie and Rosie agreed enthusiastically, and they all hurried to the door.

Outside, it was already quite light. But when Queenie, Beaver and Rosie arrived at 221b Baker Street, the house was still asleep. Even on the street itself there were few people about, only the lamplighter with his pole, putting out the gas lamps, and two or three shopkeepers returning from the markets at Covent Garden, Smithfield and Billingsgate, with the day's supply of fresh fruit and vegetables, meat and fish.

As Queenie tugged at the brass bell pull beside the door, a sweeper came round the corner with his handcart, brush and shovel, clearing up the manure dropped by the horses that had passed that way the previous day. He stopped to look at the unusual sight of three ragged urchins trying to get into a respectable house. They could hear the jangling of the bell in the hallway, but no sound of anyone coming to answer it. Queenie pulled again, and went on tugging urgently, so that the bell kept on ringing without a pause, until the door was finally opened. They were faced by a bleary-eyed Billy, wearing a nightshirt and with his hair standing up in messy spikes.

His face fell as he saw who was there. "Oh, no! Not you lot!" he said crossly. "I told you before, Mr Holmes is not here."

"We know that," Beaver told him, pushing past into the hallway.

"Oi!" Billy protested. "What you doing? You can't come in here."

"Dr Watson. We gotta see Dr Watson," Rosie cried, following Beaver in through the door.

"Now!" Queenie added firmly, following Rosie.

"He ain't up yet," Billy replied snootily. "He's still in bed, like all decent folk oughta be at this time of day."

"Then go and wake him up," demanded Beaver.

"I can't do that. You'll have to come back later."

"No! It'll be too late," Beaver shouted. "Go on!"

"I can't. It's more than my job's worth."

"It'll be more than your life's worth if you don't," Queenie threatened him.

"Listen – if you're not out of here in one minute," Billy threatened in reply, "I'll call a policeman."

"Good!" she replied. "Just make sure you get Inspector Lestrade. We need him."

Billy gawped at Queenie in surprise as she headed for the stairs.

"Come on," she said to her companions, "we'll find him ourselves."

Queenie was stopped by a stern voice from the landing.

"What's going on down there?" It was Dr Watson, wrapping his dressing gown round him as he peered over the banister. "Don't you know what time it is?"

"Doctor! We gotta talk to you!" Beaver called out breathlessly.

"Can't it wait?"

"No, Doctor," Queenie said. "It's urgent."

"It's Mr Holmes," Rosie added. "Matter of life and death."

"Ah! You'd better come up at once," the Doctor

said. He watched them climb the stairs, then called down, "Billy! Bring us a pot of tea, if you please."

"Yes, Doctor."

"Oh, and Billy – get some clothes on, there's a good chap."

Wiggins led Sparrow, Shiner and Gertie back to HQ as fast as they could go. When they got there, he grabbed Dick Turpin from the shelf and tipped the jug's contents out onto the table. It made a small pile of pennies, halfpennies and farthings; a few sixpences, threepenny bits and shillings; and a solitary half-crown.

"I hope there's enough," Wiggins said, as he scooped up the coins and put them into his pocket. "D'you know how much it is to Windsor?" he asked Shiner.

Shiner knew a lot about trains, and even about the timetables into and out of Paddington, but he had never thought about fares. When he was an engine driver, he wouldn't need to buy a ticket. He shook his head. "Dunno," he said. "I know I'm hungry, though."

"You're always hungry," Wiggins replied.

"And me," Sparrow joined in. "I'm starvin'. I need some brekker."

"No time," Wiggins said. He opened the food cupboard. It was empty apart from two rusty tins and the end of a loaf of bread. He picked up the bread, tore it in two and gave one piece each to the two boys.

"There," he said. "That's all there is. You'll have to eat it as we go. Come on." And he headed for the door.

Shiner bit into his crust at once, grumbling that it was stale, and dashed out after Wiggins. Sparrow hesitated, then tore his crust in two and gave half to Gertie, who hadn't said anything but looked hungry. She rewarded him with a smile. They followed Wiggins and Shiner out, down the passage to the street, and off, running, towards Paddington Station.

Billy brought a pot of tea and four cups on a tray, which he placed carefully on the table in front of Dr Watson.

"I'm sorry it's taken a while, sir," he apologized. "I had to get the fire going."

He did not look happy to be serving the Boys, and was not his usual smart self. He had dressed hurriedly, and had missed one of the many buttons on his jacket, so that it was fastened crookedly across his chest. He had tried to comb his hair, but it still stuck up untidily, and there was a black coal smudge on the end of his nose.

"Ah, Billy," Dr Watson greeted him. "No time for that now, I'm afraid."

"Sir?"

"We need to get to Scotland Yard as quickly as possible. Not a minute to lose. Run down to the street and get us a cab. Fast as you can!"

Pausing only to look daggers at the Boys, Billy did as he was told, and a short while later was holding open the door of a four-wheeler for them.

"Thank you, Billy," Queenie said, as she climbed aboard, nodding graciously to him like a grand lady.

Billy scowled and slammed the door behind her, and then they were off, bowling through the streets towards the police headquarters, with Dr Watson urging the driver to make haste.

* * *

Paddington Station was already starting to get busy with the morning traffic as Wiggins and his group arrived, panting and breathless, at the ticket office.

"Four tickets to Windsor, please," Wiggins gasped.

The clerk regarded him over his glasses. "Are they for you?" he asked sternly.

"Yeah, course they are," Wiggins said. "I got the money – look." He dug the coins out of his pocket and piled them on the counter.

The man stared at the money, then at Wiggins. "How old are you?"

"I don't— Fourteen?"

"Pity," the man said. "Under fourteen you only need a half fare."

Wiggins thought hard. "They ain't fourteen yet," he said, indicating the others.

"I can see that."

"And I might only be thirteen. I ain't sure."

"Then you might be fifteen. If I sold you a half-fare ticket and you were fifteen, I could be in trouble with the inspector."

"Never mind, then. Just give me the tickets."

Wiggins pushed the money across the counter.

"Right. One and three halves it is," the clerk said, and started to count the money. "Going to see Her Majesty the Queen?"

"Yeah. We're in a hurry."

The man finished counting. He looked up and shook his head. "There's only enough here for three halves."

Wiggins was stunned. He didn't know what to do, and time was running out.

"Well?" the clerk asked. "Do you want them? I haven't got all day, you know."

While Wiggins tried to make up his mind, Shiner pushed forward. The man recognized him and even managed a small smile.

"Hello, young Shiner. What are you doing here? Having a day off with your chums?"

"Yeah," Shiner answered. "We'll take the three halves."

Wiggins started to protest, but Shiner shut him up with a swift kick on the shin. He picked up the three tickets and the few pennies change, then grabbed hold of Wiggins's sleeve and pulled him away.

"What you playing at?" Wiggins demanded furiously. "You can't go without me."

"Nor will we. This way. Quick!"

He led Wiggins and the others out of the ticket office and round the side of the station, past a line of luggage trolleys.

"In here," he told Wiggins, pushing open a door. "You two stop here and keep cavey, right?"

"Where we going?"

"Porters' room. Come on."

They were only inside for a few moments. When they came out again, Wiggins had swapped his billycock hat and old coat for a porter's cap and jacket, which they had found hanging on a hook. He grabbed one of the trolleys.

"Right," said Shiner, grinning. "Platform 7."

They hurried across the station concourse, Wiggins following a little behind the others. While they were having their tickets clipped at the barrier, he pushed his trolley purposefully through the gate, like a real porter. Halfway down the platform, he paused and leant on the trolley, watching as the other Boys found an empty compartment and piled in. A minute later, the guard blew his whistle and waved his green flag to the driver. As the train began to pull out, Shiner and the others held open the door. Wiggins jumped aboard, and they were on their way.

A RACE AGAINST TIME

Just being on the train was so exciting that for the moment the Boys quite forgot how urgent their journey was. Luckily they had been able to get a compartment to themselves, so they were free to explore and investigate it. They bounced up and down on the padded seats. They stared in wonder at the framed photographs of seaside resorts screwed to the walls above the seats, and at their own faces in the narrow mirrors fixed between the pictures.

Wiggins thought he looked very good in the porter's cap, and the others laughed when he tilted it rakishly over one eye, like a fashionable young man-about-town. Gertie, however, was so shocked at the sight of her shaggy, scraggy, red hair and the hundreds of freckles on her nose and face that she screwed her eyes tight shut and refused to look again.

Sparrow was not interested in how he looked – he had seen himself many times in dressing-room mirrors at the theatre. He was having fun climbing up into the luggage rack, which was like a long net above the pictures and mirrors. When he lay down in it, he could pretend to be a sailor in a hammock, though it really wasn't very comfortable.

Shiner was the most excited of them all. He could hardly believe that he was on a train at last, and he pressed his face against the window, staring out at the railway world sliding past. First they passed other trains steaming slowly into the station at the end of their journeys. Then the goods yard and the sidings, where small shunting engines huffed and puffed and pulled carriages and freight wagons. They steamed past the tall signal box, where Shiner could see men heaving at long levers to operate the signals above the track, and the "points" that moved whole sections of rail to switch trains from one line to another. For Shiner, this was heaven.

As the train picked up speed, the sound of the wheels changed to a regular "clickety-click, clackety-clack". Shiner discovered how to lower the window in the door by releasing the leather strap that held it up, and stuck his head out to try and see the engine. He was thrilled by the feel of the wind on his face, and the sight of the trailing plume of smoke and steam. Suddenly there was a loud "whoosh", and the whole carriage shook as another train roared past in the opposite direction. Shiner let out a yelp of pain and fell back into the carriage, clapping one hand over his left eye.

"What happened?" Gertie asked, rushing to his side. "Did it hit you?"

"If it had," Wiggins laughed, "it would have knocked his block clean off."

"Ow, ow! Don't laugh – it hurts!" Shiner moaned.

"Here, let's have a look." Wiggins gently pulled Shiner's hand away, and peered into his eye. "You've got a speck of dirt in your eye from the engine."

"A speck? Blimey, it feels like a dirty great rock."

Wiggins pulled out his handkerchief, rolled one corner into a point and used it to fish out a tiny piece of black grit. "There you are," he said, showing it to Shiner. "There's your rock. You ain't gonna go blind yet awhile. Next time, just be more careful, right?"

He pointed to a sign painted over the door: "DO NOT LEAN OUT OF THE WINDOW".

Shiner, whose reading was not very good at the best of times, nodded miserably, clutching his sore eye, which was red and watering. There were obviously plenty of things he still had to learn about trains.

Soon they had left the outskirts of London and were passing through open country. The last traces of the city's fog vanished and the air was clear and fresh. Shiner and Sparrow had never seen green fields before, and were completely amazed by them. The biggest open spaces they knew were Regent's Park and Hyde Park in London, but this was something very different. These fields seemed to go on for ever, with just an occasional farmhouse or village sitting quietly amid the peace of the countryside. The few people they saw were all at work, usually with giant carthorses pulling wagons or strange pieces of agricultural equipment, and not strolling at their leisure, like the people in the parks.

When they saw herds of black and white cows and the flocks of woolly sheep, the two boys shrieked with delight. But Gertie stayed very quiet, gazing out of the window with a sad face.

"What's up, Gertie?" Wiggins asked, noticing a tear rolling down her cheek.

"Reminds me of me dad," she sniffed. "We used to live in the country when I was little."

Shiner and Sparrow stared at her in awe. Gertie had never said much about her past. Almost the only thing any of them knew about her was that her father was an Irishman, who'd had to go away.

"In the country?" Sparrow asked. "Honest?"

"Honest."

"What was it like?" Shiner asked. "Was it scary? All them animals?"

Gertie laughed. "No," she said. "There was lots

of trees to climb, and rivers and lakes to swim in. It was smashin'."

"Did you live on a farm?"

"No, in a caravan. We was always on the move."

The two younger boys were green with envy.

"Why don't you still live in a caravan, then?" Sparrow wanted to know. He couldn't imagine why anyone would give up such a life.

"The coppers took me dad away and locked him up in prison. They wanted to lock me up as well, in an orphanage. So I run away."

The others nodded sympathetically. This was something they could understand. But before they could think too much about it, they were interrupted by a shout from Wiggins.

"Look!" he cried, pointing through the window.

There, on the distant skyline, they saw the outline of a great building. A wide, circular tower, with roofs and turrets stretching away to either side of it behind a long stone wall. They could just make out a flag, flying above the tower on a tall flagpole. Windsor Castle!

*　　*　　*

A few minutes later, the train pulled into a station and stopped.

"Slough. This is Slough," a man's voice announced. "Change here for Windsor!"

"This is us. Everybody out!" Wiggins opened the door and they all poured out onto the platform. Wiggins grabbed the first porter he saw – a large man with a red face.

"Windsor. Where's the train for Windsor?" he asked.

"There ain't one, mate," the man replied. "Not this morning, anyroad."

"But we gotta get there. Quick. It's a matter of life and death."

"Oh, is it?" The man grinned at Wiggins's eagerness. "You'll have to run, then. Line's closed till the Queen's opened the new station. Ain't you heard about that?"

"Course we have. That's why we gotta get there! Somebody's trying to blow her up!"

"And you're gonna stop 'em? A porter and three kids?" He started laughing. "That's the funniest thing I've heard in years!"

"I ain't a porter."

"And we ain't just kids," Shiner shouted.

"We're the Baker Street Boys," said Sparrow.

"And we work for Mr Sherlock Holmes!" Gertie added.

The porter laughed even harder. "Ooh," he cackled. "And I'm the prime minister. This gets better and better. 'Ere, Charlie," he called to another porter, "come and 'ave a listen to this. Fair beats the music hall, this does."

"It's true. It's all true, I tell you," Wiggins protested. "If we don't get to Windsor Station in time, they'll kill the Queen."

"And Mr Holmes," Sparrow cried.

When the porter laughed again, Shiner screamed with frustration and kicked him on the shin. Hard. The man let out a yell of rage and tried to grab him.

He was stopped by a loud voice, full of authority. "Biggs! Stop that at once!"

The speaker was a middle-aged man with curly, grey side-whiskers, wearing a shiny top hat, a black frock-coat and striped trousers. He was advancing along the platform, accompanied by two burly policemen, one of them with a sergeant's stripes on his sleeve.

He pointed at the Boys and beckoned them imperiously. "You!" he ordered. "Come here."

"Oh, blimey," Shiner muttered. "The Stationmaster! Now we're for it. They know you never had no ticket, Wiggins."

"And pinched that uniform," Sparrow chipped in.

"Borrowed," Wiggins corrected him.

"Quickly, now!" the Stationmaster continued. "Is your name Wiggins?"

"Yes, sir."

"I thought so. Inspector Lestrade of Scotland Yard telegraphed me. He's coming on the next train, and we're to give you every assistance."

"They did it!" Wiggins beamed at the other Boys. "Beaver and Queenie and Rosie – they did it!"

"You need to get to Windsor, right?"

"Yeah. And fast. But that porter says there ain't no trains."

"That's right. We can't get you there by train. It's a single-track line, you see, and the royal train is already in the new station."

"We're done for, then. We ain't got time to walk."

"Never mind that," the Stationmaster said firmly. "Come along with me. Hurry now. Right, Sergeant, Constable."

He turned on his heel and marched out of the station as briskly as his dignity would allow. The Boys and the policemen followed. Outside, the Boys' mouths dropped open in amazement. Standing at the entrance were two gleaming motor cars, each with a driver wearing peaked cap and goggles at the wheel. The car engines were ticking over, ready to go.

"Don't stand there gawping!" the Stationmaster bellowed, waving them forward with both hands. "Have you never seen a horseless carriage before? Get aboard! No time to lose! Get aboard!"

The Boys needed no second bidding. What a day this was turning out to be! They scrambled into the first car – Wiggins in front by the driver, the other three in the rear seat – while the Stationmaster and the two policemen climbed into the second car.

"Full speed ahead, drivers!" the Stationmaster

shouted, exchanging his top hat for a baggy cap with flaps, which he fastened under his chin. "To Windsor – and don't spare the horsepower! A sovereign for the first across the bridge!"

The drivers tooted their horns and engaged forward gear, and the race was on. Through the little town they sped, forcing pedestrians to leap on to the pavements for safety, scaring old ladies, frightening horses and rousing sleeping dogs who rushed into the road after them, barking furiously. For the Boys, this was even more exciting than the train ride. They clung on for dear life as their car rattled and shook over the cobbled streets.

Once they were clear of the town, they trailed a huge cloud of dust behind them from the unmade road. As the car following had to drive through this, the policemen's uniforms quickly turned from blue to grey. Coughing and spluttering, the Stationmaster grabbed the top of the windscreen, half stood up in his seat and urged his driver to overtake. But the road was too narrow and the Boys' driver too determined, and so they stayed in front. Ahead of them, the distant bulk of the castle grew steadily bigger and bigger as they got nearer. To one side, across the fields, they could see the railway line, raised on a long row of brick arches, leading to the foot of the castle.

Soon they were entering another small town. The castle towered over the far end of its High Street, divided from it by a wide river. To the Boys' astonishment, the streets were filled with boys, wearing shiny top hats, striped trousers, short black "bum-freezer" jackets and big, stiff, white collars. They were all heading towards the bridge that crossed the river. The cars had to slow down to avoid hitting them.

Wiggins leant over to the driver. "Is this Windsor?" he asked.

"No," the man told him. "Windsor's the other side of the river. This is Eton, where the toffs go to school."

"Cor, fancy having to dress up like that every day to go to school!"

"Out of the way! Get out of the way!" the driver yelled, tooting his horn frantically. But the large number of schoolboys and other people in the street slowed the car to a crawl. By the time the cars had reached the tollgate on the other side of the bridge, they were forced to stop.

"It's no good," the driver said. "Too many people going to see the Queen."

The other car had pulled up behind them. The Stationmaster and the two policemen jumped out, dusted themselves down and hurried over.

"It'll be quicker on foot!" the Stationmaster shouted. "And anyway, the motors would never make it up the hill. This way! Come on!"

The Boys clambered out and followed him onto the bridge, pushing through the crowd.

"What's this river?" Wiggins asked as they crossed.

The Stationmaster looked at him as though he were stupid. "Why, the Thames, of course," he said.

The Boys stared over the side of the ancient stone bridge at the clear water running below. It did not look much like the great, grimy waterway that flowed through London, bustling with tugs and barges and river traffic. Led by the Stationmaster and the policemen, all puffing heavily, Wiggins and the Boys hurried across the bridge, then along the promenade that ran alongside the river. The boats here all seemed to be pleasure craft – launches and skiffs and dinghies. A hundred yards upstream another, more modern, iron bridge with two boats moored underneath it carried the railway across. It made a peaceful scene, but there was no time to stand and admire it.

The little party turned into the steep street that led up from the river, under the shadow of the immense outer wall of the castle. The shops facing the castle were gaily decorated with bunting and flags. So, too, was the entrance to the new station at the top of the slope, where guardsmen in their red tunics and tall, black bearskin hats lined the pavements. The Boys felt very important as they hurried between them onto the station concourse, where a military band was playing rousing tunes.

"Well, we're here," the Stationmaster said. "What now?"

"I dunno," Wiggins replied. "I don't… Wait a minute – yes, I do. Look!"

He pointed to a tall figure among the crowd. It was the American with the broad, black hat and the heavy moustache.

"Sergeant," he said urgently. "That's our man. That's the leader of the gang."

"Is it indeed?" the Sergeant replied. "Right."

The Stationmaster drew in his breath sharply. "He looks a nasty piece of work," he warned. "You'd best take care."

The Sergeant nodded. "You stay here," he told the Boys. "Out of harm's way. I'll get reinforcements."

He and the Constable moved quietly to the edge of the crowd, summoning two other policemen from the pavement to join them. The Boys watched as they slipped behind the spectators, then approached the big man from either side. A moment later, they had seized his arms and were leading him away to the station office.

"Excellent!" the Stationmaster declared. "Very well done. Come along, boys. Let's see what the villain has to say for himself."

*   *   *

In the station office, the big man, who was now in handcuffs, was protesting vigorously in a strong American accent, "Lemme loose, you numbskulls! You don't know what you're getting involved in!"

"Oh yes, we do," said Wiggins. And then continued in his best Sherlock Holmes voice, "The game's up! You might as well come clean."

The man stared at him as though he were mad. "Who is this kid? And what's he talking about?"

"We know you're in league with the Professor to blow up the Queen and Mr Holmes."

"Mr Holmes? Mr Sherlock Holmes?"

"Exac'ly. Now, where's the bomb?"

"That's what I'm trying to find out, stupid! I'm not a terrorist – I'm a detective."

They all stared at him in complete disbelief.

"My name is Thaddeus T. Judd, of the Pinkerton Detective Agency in the United States of America. Kindly feel in my inside pocket, Sergeant – and look sharp about it."

He raised his hands to show that he could not do it himself because of the handcuffs. The Sergeant did as he was asked, and produced a small, black leather wallet, which contained a silver badge and an identity card, which he read quickly.

"He's telling the truth," he said.

"You're not a terrorist?" Wiggins asked, amazed by this sudden turn of events.

"No, I'm not. Your terrorists are still out there – with their bomb."

SAVING THE QUEEN

"I've been tracking these guys all the way from Boston, Massachusetts, in the US of A," Thaddeus T. Judd explained, as the sergeant released him from the handcuffs. "The Boston police chief called in my agency to help catch them. They are Fenians and they've come over here to cause mischief."

"What are Fenians?" Wiggins asked.

"It's another name for the Irish Brotherhood," Judd explained. "They're revolutionaries and crooks."

"And murderers," the Sergeant added meaningfully.

"And they want to kill Her Majesty the Queen?" the Stationmaster asked, deeply shocked.

"Looks like it," Judd replied.

"And Mr Holmes," said Wiggins.

"I don't know about that. But I sure wouldn't put it past them."

"Then we must stop them!" the Stationmaster exclaimed. "Where are they now?"

"That, sir, is the hundred-dollar question. I've hunted through every inch of this station, and I can't see any trace of them, and no sign of any bomb, either."

"But they must be here somewhere," the Sergeant said, pushing back his helmet and scratching his head. "Where else would they be?"

Wiggins had begun pacing up and down the room, thinking hard. Now he stopped and held up one hand. "Half a mo," he said sharply. "Sparrow, tell me again what you heard 'em saying. Besides the bit about the grand opening going with a bang."

"Well," said Sparrow, "there was all that about a train and the widow…"

"Yes, yes. Go on!"

"Oh, yeah, there was that bit we couldn't work out, about over the water…"

"That's it!" Wiggins's face lit up. "Over the

water – over the river, more like!"

"I don't get it," Judd said.

"What goes over the river?" Wiggins yelled excitedly.

"Why, a bridge, I guess."

"Exac'ly!" Wiggins turned to the other Boys. "When we was running along the river from Eton, there was another bridge close by."

"Yes. The railway bridge," the Stationmaster said.

"Right. And I saw two boats under that bridge. One was a posh steamboat with a funnel and all; the other was a rowing boat. And I noticed there was a bloke sitting in it, on his own."

"So?"

"When there's all this going on up here, with the Queen and everything, why would anybody want to sit in a boat, underneath the railway bridge, where you can't see nothing?"

"By golly!" Judd gasped. "The kid's right! They're going to blow up the bridge as the royal train passes over it."

"We gotta get down there!" Wiggins yelled. "Quick! Come on, everybody!"

"The quickest way is along the track," the Stationmaster cried, flinging open the office door.

With Wiggins and the Boys leading, the whole party rushed out and raced past an astonished line of dignitaries who were waiting by the royal train, its sparkling green and gold locomotive gently letting off steam in readiness. At the end of the platform, they hopped down onto the track and ran along it. Behind them, they heard the band strike up the National Anthem, a sign that the Queen had arrived at the station.

The Boys, being younger and fitter, soon left everyone else behind. The track curved sharply to the right, and they could see the river and the metal bridge about two hundred yards ahead, where the town gave way to fields and the tow-path was lined with bushes. The bridge looked like two giant silver coat-hangers laid above the water on brick pillars, carrying the track between them. The tops of the two metal arches were decorated for the occasion with Union Jack flags and golden crowns.

The steamboat that Wiggins had noticed was pulling out and steaming away fast downstream.

In the stern stood the two Fenians, grinning as they looked back towards the bridge. At the wheel was a gaunt figure Wiggins recognized as Professor Moriarty, wearing a white yachting cap and a grim smile of satisfaction. The other, smaller, boat was still moored under the bridge. The solitary man was sitting upright in its centre, gagged and tied up with rope. He turned his head, and Wiggins saw with horror that it was Sherlock Holmes.

In a few seconds, the Boys were on the bridge, looking down at the river and the bow of the boat, about fifteen feet below.

"Hang on, Mr Holmes!" Wiggins shouted, "We're coming!"

"Yeah, but how d'we get down?" Sparrow asked.

"Jump!" said Gertie, clambering onto the parapet.

"I can't swim," Wiggins admitted.

"Nor me," wailed Sparrow and Shiner in unison.

"I can," said Gertie, launching herself into the air.

She landed with a splash, struck out swiftly for

the boat and hauled herself aboard.

"Don't fret, Mr Holmes!" she said, pulling the gag from his mouth. "The Baker Street Boys is here. Soon have you untied."

"Never mind about me," Mr Holmes told her. "You must deal with that first."

He turned his eyes upwards. Gertie followed his gaze, and saw a bundle of sticks of dynamite tied to a girder on the underside of the bridge. A fuse dangled from it, sizzling and sparking – it had already burned dangerously low.

"Can you climb to it?" Mr Holmes demanded.

"Me, sir? I can climb anythin'," she answered, and in an instant was shinning up the lattice-work of the bridge with all the agility of a monkey. As Gertie approached the bundle of dynamite, Wiggins appeared and started clambering awkwardly down the side of the bridge.

"Pull the fuse out!" he yelled at her.

"That's what I *am* doin'!" she shouted back.

Gertie yanked the fuse free, and threw it into the river, where it fizzled briefly and went out.

In the silence that followed, they heard a train whistle, a puffing and hissing, and then a heavy rumble as the royal train passed over their heads. The Queen was safely on her way to London.

Sherlock Holmes looked up and gave them a grateful smile. "Well done," he said. "Very well done, my Boys."

Inspector Lestrade, Beaver, Queenie, Rosie and Dr Watson were waiting for the rescuers in the station office when they returned with Mr Holmes, who seemed none the worse for his ordeal.

"Holmes!" Dr Watson burst out, with some emotion. "Are you all right?"

"Never better, my dear fellow. Thanks to my splendid Irregulars."

"Yes, indeed. They have been truly splendid."

"The whole country owes them a great debt of gratitude," the Stationmaster boomed. "I shall make it my business to see that their service is properly recognized."

"I fear that may not be," Mr Holmes replied. "They shall certainly be rewarded, but this whole affair must remain a closely guarded secret. Her Majesty must never know of the plot to murder her."

"Quite so," Dr Watson agreed. "It would break her heart."

"And the British public would be alarmed to learn how close the villains came to succeeding," Holmes continued.

"Not to mention how they managed to out-smart our greatest detective," Lestrade added, with a hint of sarcasm in his voice.

"And Scotland Yard," Mr Holmes responded, with a cool smile.

"And the Pinkerton Detective Agency, I have to admit," Judd said ruefully. "Let's face it, gentle-men, the kids are the only ones who got it right."

"Even though we did have you down as a vil-lain," Wiggins said, grinning.

"Well, I guess I can't blame you, the way I look," the big American said, fingering the scar on his face. "Though sometimes it helps to look tough when you're dealing with crooks and gangsters."

"Speaking of which," Dr Watson said, "how did Professor Moriarty come to be involved in all this?"

"An excellent question, Watson. Wiggins, my young friend," Mr Holmes said, turning to him.

"You appear to have been one step ahead of the rest of us in this business. Do you have any ideas?"

Wiggins thought for a moment then said, "The way I see it is this: the Professor is Mr Holmes's sworn enemy – Mr Holmes has beat him in the past, right?"

"Right," Mr Holmes affirmed. "Go on."

"So he wants to get his own back. Like, revenge. He hears that these Fenian geezers are plotting to kill the Queen ... he might even have put 'em up to it."

"A good point. Excellent. And?"

"He reckons if he can trap Mr Holmes, instead of just killing him – what would be too easy for a clever bloke like the Professor – he can make it look like he was in on the plot. And that way, he won't have just done him in, he'll have ruined his good name as well. Everybody'd think he'd gone wrong, and remember him as a bad egg."

"Bravo, Wiggins!" Sherlock Holmes cried. "I could not have put it better myself."

"Well, I never!" Dr Watson was amazed.

"Fiendish! Truly fiendish!" Lestrade exclaimed.

Wiggins grinned from ear to ear, and the other Boys gazed at him in admiration.

"What I don't understand," said Beaver, frowning heavily, "is why they had that funny door. Why couldn't they have had just a good lock and key?"

"Wiggins?" Mr Holmes asked.

Wiggins looked perplexed, and shook his head.

"I mean," Beaver went on, "it was bound to get noticed."

"Precisely," said Mr Holmes, tilting his head enquiringly at Wiggins.

After a moment Wiggins's face cleared.

"Oh, I get it," he said. "Bait!"

"Well done, Wiggins. You're going to make a fine detective one day. It was indeed bait for the trap. Moriarty knew I would get to hear of the strange door – indeed, he made sure I did by having one of his associates engage me to follow Mr Judd in the belief that he was up to no good. Moriarty guessed that I would be drawn to that door to discover its purpose and who was using it. Once they had me in that alleyway, they were able to overpower me with a liberal dose of chloroform."

"The brutes!" Dr Watson cried.

"Better than cracking my skull with a blow to the head."

"But how did you manage to leave a trail, if you was knocked out?" Rosie asked.

"Ah, the matches!" Mr Holmes smiled at her. "You spotted them."

"*I* did," she said proudly. "And I smelled the chlorywhatsit, but I didn't know what it was then."

"Well done. Very well done. When I first caught a whiff of the drug, I was able to resist its effects for a little while by holding my breath. Long enough to spill a box-full of matches from my tray as they were dragging me inside."

"Good job you did," Wiggins told him. "Else we wouldn't have known where you was."

"I knew I could rely on my Irregulars," Mr Holmes replied.

"I guess I have to take the blame for leading you into his trap," Judd admitted. "I was so intent on tracking those two Fenians, I never thought there might be another side to it."

"No need to reproach yourself on that score, my friend," Mr Holmes responded generously. "Moriarty's fiendish cunning has outwitted better men than you."

"Well, he sure made a fool outta me."

"And indeed out of me. I must confess that I stepped right into his snare. He is certainly a worthy opponent, but he failed to include one important factor in his calculations: my brilliant assistants."

"Hurrah!" the Stationmaster cried. "Hurrah for the Baker Street Boys!"

And the adults in the room all cheered loudly.

A moment later, there was a knock at the door and the Sergeant entered. "Good news!" he announced. "The villains' steamboat has been intercepted at the next lock down the river. My officers have apprehended two men, and taken them into custody."

"Congratulations, sir!" the Stationmaster called out.

"Well done, Sergeant," said Lestrade.

Sherlock Holmes held up his hand. "Two men, you say?"

"Yes, sir. The Fenians, undoubtedly."

"And the third man?" Mr Holmes asked.

"There was no third man aboard the launch, sir. Only the two Fenians."

"I see." Mr Holmes nodded calmly, the ghost of a smile flickering across his lips. "So," he continued, "he lives to fight another day. Well, we shall see. For the moment, anyway, we may celebrate another victory."

The Boys travelled back to London in the luxury of a first class carriage, with a large hamper of delicious refreshments to eat and drink on the way. Apart from Shiner, that is, who rode on the footplate of the engine, along with the driver and fireman, and was even allowed to pull levers and turn wheels and sound the train's whistle as they passed through towns and villages. It was a journey he wished would never end.

Later, after a sumptuous feast provided by Mr Holmes, they were fitted out with new clothes, which Queenie said were far too good for every day and must be kept for special occasions.

The first special occasion was that very

evening, when they were taken to a West End variety theatre, where they sat in the best seats to watch the show. They all enjoyed every minute of it, laughing and clapping and cheering, and joining in the songs. But Sparrow enjoyed it most of all, for the star of the show, at the top of the bill, was his hero, Little Tich.

After so much excitement, some of the Boys found it hard to sleep that night. Queenie woke up sometime in the small hours, and left her bed to get a drink of water from the big stone jar that they kept near the stove. She found Beaver sitting on his own at the table, with a furrowed brow, writing something by the light of a candle. The tip of his tongue poked out of the side of his mouth and he was concentrating so hard that he did not hear her until she spoke. When she did, he jumped violently.

"Beaver?" she asked. "What you doin'?"

He looked up a little sheepishly. "Thought I'd try and write down all what's happened these last couple of days. Like Dr Watson does for Mr Holmes."

"That's a good idea," Queenie said. "Have you got a name for it?"

Beaver sucked his pencil for a minute, thinking hard. Then he grinned. "Yeah," he said. "I think I'll call it 'The Case of the Disappearing Detective'."

BAKER STREET

SHERLOCK HOLMES, the famous detective, was invented in 1887 by Sir Arthur Conan Doyle, who wrote no fewer than sixty stories about him. Sir Arthur gave Holmes and his friend Dr John Watson rooms at number 221b Baker Street, London, which has since become one of the best-known addresses in the whole world.

The Baker Street Boys – or the Baker Street Irregulars, as Sherlock Holmes sometimes called them – were mentioned in the very first story and in three others. Their leader, Wiggins, was the only one to be given a name by Conan Doyle. The other children have all been created by Anthony Read for this series of original adventures.

WINDSOR ROYAL STATION

WINDSOR STATION was rebuilt in 1897 by the Great Western Railway Company to mark Queen Victoria's Diamond Jubilee, when she celebrated sixty years on the throne of Great Britain. It is now a shopping centre known as Windsor Royal Station, but trains still run from it, and still cross the bridge over the River Thames that is featured in this story. A full-size replica of the railway engine that pulled Queen Victoria's royal train stands in the middle of the station.

A SHOW-STOPPER
OF A MYSTERY!

Starring
Mystic Marvin
and Little Mary

With a supporting cast of
The Baker Street Boys:
London's boldest, bravest
street-urchin detectives!

Mystic Marvin and Little Mary
are a popular act at the Imperial
Music Hall. But if Mary's hypnotic
trance isn't real, why is she acting
so strangely? Sparrow decides
to find out – and discovers
that all is not as it seems...

**With Sherlock Holmes out of
town, only the Baker Street
Boys can save the day!**

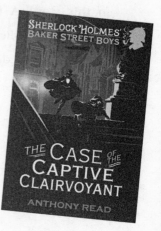

ROLL UP, ROLL UP!

Hurry to see Madame Dupont's famous waxworks

A DISPLAY *MAGNIFIQUE*!

Now showing:

THE RAJA OF RANJIPUR
and his priceless ruby...

When the Baker Street Boys rescue a young Indian prince from murderous thugs, they become involved in a dangerous intrigue. Can they solve the string of mysterious deaths that surround their new friend?

With Sherlock Holmes out of town, only the Baker Street Boys can save the day!

SINISTER HAPPENINGS AFOOT!

Flower Girls Disappearing in Broad Daylight!

The Baker Street Boys are on a wild-goose chase ... or should that be a DRAGON chase?

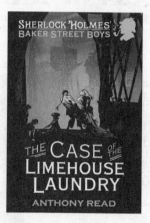

Rosie has been kidnapped, and the Boys are on the case. But their only lead is a puzzling clue from Sparrow's Chinese friends. Can there *really* be a dragon in London? And how will it lead them to Rosie?

With Sherlock Holmes out of town, only the Baker Street Boys can save the day!

STOLEN:
THE MOUNTJOY DIAMONDS...

**Thief on the loose!
Could it be
an inside job?**

**A gem of a case for
the Baker Street Boys!**

Lady Mountjoy's diamonds
are missing and Polly, her
maid, is wrongly accused of
the theft. The Baker Street
Boys agree to help her find
the real culprit ... but soon
realize that everyone has
something to hide.

**With Sherlock Holmes out of town, only the
Baker Street Boys can save the day!**

BRAND-NEW EXHIBITION!

The Dungeon of Horrors:
A MOST TERRIFYING AND GRUESOME DISPLAY

Prepare to be scared. Very, very scared.

Wiggins and Beaver get a fright when they visit Madame Dupont's new exhibition – but that's just the beginning. Before long they're caught up in a Russian spy ring and a case of mistaken identity...

With Sherlock Holmes out of town, only the Baker Street Boys can save the day!

Fancy a Flutter?

Take a punt on Silver Star,
the **2/1 favourite**
for the **3:20 at Ally Pally!**

But, wait! All is not as it seems...
What are the odds Moriarty's involved?

Gertie's father stands accused of murder, and if she can't prove his innocence, he'll be hanged! The Boys go undercover at Major Lee's racing stables to do some digging around. But what will they find...?

With Sherlock Holmes out of town, only the Baker Street Boys can save the day!

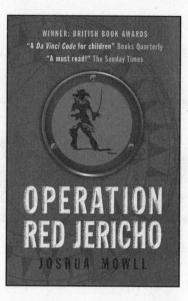

WINNER: BRITISH BOOK AWARDS
"A *Da Vinci Code* for children" Books Quarterly
"A must read!" The Sunday Times

OPERATION RED JERICHO
JOSHUA MOWLL

Shanghai 1920: while on board the *Expedient*, Doug and Becca MacKenzie anxiously await news of their missing parents ... and stumble across a far greater mystery.

England 2002: Joshua Mowll inherits a remarkable archive of documents and painstakingly pieces together the extraordinary events that took place over eighty years earlier.

This is the story of a mysterious Guild striving to protect an ancient secret; the story of two young people caught up in an astonishing adventure ... with far-reaching consequences for the whole world.

**Operation Red Jericho.
No ordinary tale: no ordinary book.**

THE FLAXFIELD QUARTET:

The final book, *Starborn*, coming soon!

ANTHONY READ studied at the Central School of Speech and Drama in London, and was an actor-manager at the age of eighteen. He worked in advertising, journalism and publishing and as a BAFTA-winning television producer before becoming a full-time writer. Anthony has more than two hundred screen credits to his name, for programmes that include *Sherlock Holmes*, *The Professionals* and *Doctor Who*. He has also written non-fiction, and won the Wingate Literary Prize for *Kristallnacht*.

The seven Baker Street Boys books are based on Anthony's original television series for children, broadcast by the BBC in the 1980s, for which he won the Writers' Guild TV Award. The series was inspired by references to the "Baker Street Irregulars", a group of young crime-solvers who helped the detective Sherlock Holmes in the classic stories by Sir Arthur Conan Doyle.